EXIT DYING

A man, elegantly ~~~~~~~~~~~~~~~,
stared at us. It w~~~~~~

We met years ago ~~~~~~~~~~~~~~ ~~~tting
for a rich lady on ~~~~~~~~~~~~ whose passion was English ~~~~~~~~~~~ He was then a
show judge and b~~~~~~~ whose love for and
knowledge of cats was proverbial. We rarely
spoke to each other more than twice a year, but
there was a genuine affection between us, and
he had a special spot in his heart for my crazy
cat, Pancho, whom he claimed was the reincarnation of one of Napoleon's generals.

I was so stunned at seeing him that all I could
say was, "John. What are you doing here?"

"John? My name is not John."

"John, it's me. Alice! Alice Nestleton."

"My name isn't John," he repeated.

I didn't know how to reply. But just then Adda
Krispus called out, "Wait!" I stopped.

"Look!" she said.

I looked. In her hand was a small pistol with a
white bone handle.

She raised it, aimed, and fired it into the face of
John Cerise. She fired five times. And then she
dropped the weapon on the chest of the fallen
man. She looked at us, smiling almost sweetly.
"Shouldn't you call the police?" she inquired . . .

A CAT IN
A CHORUS LINE

A CAT IN A
CHORUS LINE

An Alice Nestleton Mystery

Lydia Adamson

A SIGNET BOOK

SIGNET
Published by the Penguin Group
Penguin Books USA Inc., 375 Hudson Street,
New York, New York 10014, U.S.A.
Penguin Books Ltd, 27 Wrights Lane,
London W8 5TZ, England
Penguin Books Australia Ltd, Ringwood,
Victoria, Australia
Penguin Books Canada Ltd, 10 Alcorn Avenue,
Toronto, Ontario, Canada M4V 3B2
Penguin Books (N.Z.) Ltd, 182–190 Wairau Road,
Auckland 10, New Zealand

Penguin Books Ltd, Registered Offices:
Harmondsworth, Middlesex, England

First published by Signet, an imprint of Dutton Signet,
a division of Penguin Books USA Inc.

First Printing, May, 1996
10 9 8 7 6 5 4 3 2 1

The first chapter of this book previously appeared in *A Cat in Fine Style*.
Cover art by Robert Crawford

 REGISTERED TRADEMARK—MARCA REGISTRADA

Printed in the United States of America

PUBLISHER'S NOTE
This is a work of fiction. Names, characters, places, and incidents
either are the product of the author's imagination or are used
fictitiously, and any resemblance to actual persons, living or dead,
events, or locales is entirely coincidental.

Chapter 1

"I don't know why I agreed to go to this stupid party, anyway," I shouted angrily to Tony Basillio. He was rushing me. I don't like to be rushed when I'm dressing.

"One . . . we're late already, Madame Nestleton. And two . . . it's not a party."

"Then what is it?" I inquired, trying to figure out in the mirror how many buttons on my blouse I should keep open, from the top. It was a hot summer night but three buttons were a bit risque—given my age.

"Well, it's more like a charity ball."

I scoffed. "In a Hell's Kitchen tenement? No! It's an old-fashioned rent party."

"Look, Swede! The man is old and sick and broke. And he's one of ours."

"What do you mean, 'one of ours'?"

"Like us. Theater people."

I guess Tony had a point. If anyone was

"theater people," it was Peter Nelson Krispus. During the 1970s he wrote the words and music and script for three strange "operettas." Two were successful way off Broadway. One closed after four nights on Broadway. Critics either loathed him or loved him. One said he set back the musical comedy form a hundred years. Another said "Krispus is delusional. He thinks he can make a bump-and-grind vaudeville show into an art form." And the prestigious critic of the *New York Times* wrote: "Krispus has made an amazing theatrical leap. He has successfully fused Gilbert and Sullivan with Eugene Ionesco."

Now, there was nothing left of his genius, if that was what he had. He no longer wrote. His plays or operettas or *divertissements* (everyone had a different name for them) were no longer performed. And the memory of them was kept alive by a small cult of followers, mostly in academia. There was even, I had heard, a name for his style of theatrical piece—"operetta of the absurd." I had seen only one of his works. It was called, if I remember correctly, *Ending on a Dominant.* I forgot it twelve minutes after I left the theater. And the songs—lewd takeoffs on Gilbert and Sullivan—never even registered.

"We stay there only an hour or so. It gets very crowded," Tony explained.

"When do they pass the hat?" I asked.

"No hat, Swede. Just a big flowerpot on a ledge over a walled-up fireplace. People do it discreetly."

I put on the finishing touch—my grandmother's tiny jade earrings—and began opening cans to feed Bushy and Pancho, who were getting angry at my slothfulness. When they saw I was opening just plain old cat food cans they became angrier, because I had promised them Norwegian sardines with skin and bones intact.

"Learn to postpone gratification, cats," I cautioned them. Bushy looked ashamed for me, at my betrayal. He turned his head away. Pancho shortened his manic runs from imaginary enemies and began an almost stately trot, giving me the evil eye on occasion.

"Look at that lunatic cat," Tony said, shaking his head at Pancho's antics. "Now he thinks he's one of the Lippizzaners."

"Do not call Pancho a lunatic. I don't appreciate it."

"You would think that as he gets older he would get calmer. But not Pancho. He runs all day. He runs all night. A lot of people

7

Lydia Adamson

hope that whoever is chasing him will finally catch him."

"He was abused as a kitten."

Tony found that very funny. "If I know one thing," he said, "it's that Pancho was never a kitten. He sprang full blown and running out of his mother's womb."

"Of course he was a kitten . . . a cuddly little ball of gray. And then the world turned on him." It was a ridiculously dramatic line. I don't know what possessed me to utter it.

Tony applauded sardonically, then said: "I think he needs a woman."

"Who?"

"Pancho."

"He's celibate."

"It would do him good. He would have to pay attention. He would have to stop and look around."

"Do you have someone in mind?"

"In fact, Madame Nestleton, I do. I don't know her name but she lives in a cellar around Twenty-ninth and Lexington."

"A cellar?"

"Yes. A cellar. I was walking past and the cellar was open and this cat was seated about three steps down. She had those big ears and a weird shape."

"You mean a Japanese bobtail?"

"Maybe. I didn't ask her. Anyway, she had those wide eyes and spooky black pupils of cats that spend most of their lives in the dark. And she had beautiful black-and-white markings. And I said to myself, as we stared at each other, now this is the perfect woman for Pancho. I mean, perfect. Let's face it—Pancho is not much to look at and this lady in the cellar probably can't see in daylight anymore. She'd only see Pancho in the dark. Which, let's face it . . . given all his scars . . . is when he looks best."

"Make the match, Tony," I said.

Then I placed the dishes of cat food down in the usual location and got back to the real matter at hand.

"What really confuses me, Tony, is why they would have this kind of rent party in August, when all the theater people with any kind of money are out of the city."

"I think the date has some kind of significance. It's always on August twenty-first. Maybe it's someone's birthday. Or an anniversary."

Suddenly a wondrous breeze just floated across my loft. It was almost cool and very welcome, since my newly installed ceiling fan had broken down completely.

Both of my cats had already forgiven me,

forgotten their dream of sardines, and were deep into their food.

"Actually," Tony said, "I was shocked when you finally agreed to accompany me to a Krispus party."

"You shock easy."

"Why *are* you coming?"

I grinned. "Why do you think?"

"Love and compassion for me and the desire to make me happy," Tony replied nastily.

"Actually I want to see those cats," I corrected. I was talking about George Bernard and Shaw, as Krispus's two cats were named. They were silver tabby Maine coon cats and I just had to see if they were as big and beautiful as Tony claimed they were. Of course I knew in my heart that my red and cream Bushy was the biggest and most beautiful Maine coon cat of all times.

We took the bus uptown and got off at 49th Street and 8th Avenue. We walked west toward Krispus's apartment on 52nd Street and 10th Avenue. Tony grabbed my hand and held it tightly.

"Nostalgia?" I queried.

"Exactly."

This was indeed our old neighborhood. It was the neighborhood of virtually every young man and woman who came to New York to study acting.

Tony and I had met in an acting school over a theater on 52nd Street and Broadway. We hung out in a Greek coffee shop on 47th Street and 9th Avenue. We drank beer in a working-class bar on 50th and 8th.

It was growing darker and warmer. Tony was beginning to wax poetic: "Call it the theater district, call it the Great White Way, call it the Deuce, call it Hell's Kitchen; call it whatever you want, but it still has the highest concentration of theaters and Laundromats and junkies in the country. And I love it."

We reached the building where Krispus lived. It was a grimy six-story brownstone with a crumbling stoop.

The front door was propped open with an old telephone book in a pathetic attempt to coax a street breeze in.

The lock on the hallway door was long gone.

"They're on the fifth floor," Tony said.

Up we trudged.

"I don't hear any music," I noted, as we climbed.

"How many times do I have to tell you! It's not that kind of party."

Then he kissed me on the neck and halted my ascent. Whispering dramatically, he said: "Doesn't this feel like one of those old gangster movies? A tall, beautiful, golden haired woman climbs the stairs of a seedy West Side tenement. With her is the dark, ugly, flashily dressed killer."

"You're not flashily dressed, Tony," I noted and resumed the climb.

We reached the fifth floor. Tony led me to the front apartment and knocked.

I knew exactly what I would see when the door opened: a refrigerator. These long, narrow "railroad flats" always opened into the back of the apartment—the kitchen. In fact, I could visualize the whole scheme. There would be two large windows in the front that looked down on the street, and then no windows at all until you reach the back of the apartment. Then two more large windows in the kitchen, looking down on the yard. Off the kitchen would be the bathroom, with one tiny window. No partitions throughout. No separations. Yes, I knew these kinds of apartments. I had lived in enough of them.

The door swung open. I smiled. It *was* the kitchen.

Framed in the doorway was a heavyset

woman about sixty years old with enormous hips and red-gray hair frizzled all over. Her face was full of old freckles. She was smoking a cigarette in a holder. She was wearing a kimono of sorts and on her feet were sandals.

Tony said happily: "You're Mrs. Krispus. Adda Krispus."

"What do you want?" the woman replied.

Then I saw the cats. They had obviously wandered into the kitchen, curious. My heart turned one of those little flips. They were magnificent. They looked like their mother had been a lynx and their father a snow leopard. And they were huge.

"Well," mumbled a nervous and slightly embarrassed Tony, "it's always hard to be the first guests at a party."

"The party is tomorrow night," she said.

"But today is the twenty-first."

"Correct. That means tomorrow is the twenty-second. We hold the party on August twenty-second every year."

"No!" exclaimed a stubborn Tony. "On the twenty-first. I've been to them."

Adda Krispus looked at Tony as if he were a difficult child. Then she grabbed both our wrists in a friendly fashion and pulled us into the apartment.

"Look around! Do you see a party going on?"

The apartment was virtually empty of people and furniture. In the front end of the apartment, a man lay on a bed with wheels. He looked very old and very ill.

Tony was getting more and more embarrassed. He looked to me for help. I kept my eyes on the silver tabby Maine coons so I could describe them perfectly to Bushy.

"I'm truly sorry busting in here like a fool," he pleaded to Mrs. Krispus.

He grasped my hand then and began to pull me toward the door.

Then a man elegantly dressed in a white linen suit walked out of the bathroom.

He stared over at us. His face was strong, compelling—but not readily identifiable as the face of a man or a woman—there was a kind of noble androgyny to it. His dyed ebony hair was slicked back. He might have been forty years old. But then again, he might just as well have been seventy.

It took me a full ten seconds before I realized just who it was I was studying so minutely. The handsome man in the white suit was my old friend John Cerise.

We met years ago when I first started cat-sitting for a rich lady on Central Park South

14

whose passion was English shorthairs. He was then a cat show judge and breeder whose love for and knowledge of cats was proverbial. We rarely spoke to each other more than twice a year, but there was a genuine affection between us and he had a special spot in his heart for my crazy cat, Pancho, whom he claimed was the reincarnation of one of Napoleon's generals.

In a sense he was my feline guru. And we had that kind of distant intimacy one develops with gurus. I wrote him from time to time with all kinds of questions about the feline tribes—health questions, behavior questions, even philosophical questions. In short, I had developed the same kind of trusting relationship with John that I had previously reserved for old acting teachers of mine. Above all, John could be trusted. Many times he had helped me out in dangerous situations, without any thought of recompense.

I was so stunned at seeing him that all I could say was: "John. What are you doing here?"

"John? My name is not John."

I didn't know how to reply. I turned to Tony. He shrugged. I turned back to John

Cerise. What was the matter with him? Had he been hit on the head?

"John, it's me. Alice Nestleton."

"My name isn't John," he repeated.

Tony pulled my arm and whispered, "Let's go." He said it in a weary, cynical voice as if we had now *both* made fools of ourselves and it was time to leave.

We started to walk out.

"Wait!" Adda Krispus called out. We stopped.

"Look!" she said.

We looked. In her hand now was a small pistol with a white bone handle.

She raised it, aimed, and fired it into the face of John Cerise. She fired five times. And then she dropped the weapon on the chest of the fallen man. She looked at us, smiling, almost sweetly. "Shouldn't you call the police?" she inquired.

Chapter 2

Not long ago, Tony and I played a scene from the old drama, *Detective Story*. If I were a set designer working on a production of that play, I'd have a field day making the sets as grungy as possible.

Well, I am here to report that when it comes to grunge and grime, the real-life precinct at 54th Street and 8th Avenue outdoes any designer's imagination.

We were sitting on one hard wooden bench or another for hours, waiting to be interviewed by the officer in charge of the John Cerise shooting.

Basillio kept taking my hand. Time and again he would take my fingers in his, trying to comfort me.

Each time, I shook him off me.

Finally, I shoved my hand inside my pocket.

"How much longer do you think it'll be, Swede?" he said.

It wasn't the first time he had asked that question. In answer, I merely shook my head.

The station house was by turns stifling and freezing, depending on where we sat. Near the sergeant's desk, where the huge industrial fan was whirring, the cold air threatened to blow us out of our chairs. But back near the ancient water fountain it was moist and hot.

I took a long swallow of water and began, for the hundredth time, to go over in my mind what had happened that night.

Just what *had* happened? When I thought about it, some scenes went by in slow motion, others at a rapid-fire pace, triple time.

I saw myself putting on my lipstick and deciding which earrings to wear.

I saw Tony standing in my loft, jokingly describing the party we were going to attend as a charity ball.

There was something about fixing Pancho up with a tough little cat who lived in a basement somewhere.

Tony and I walking up the tenement stairs and into the Krispuses' shotgun apartment—no pun intended.

Wrong night. The party's tomorrow.

Two silver tabbies the size of yaks.

John Cerise suddenly appearing in the room.

No, he says, my name isn't John.

"Look!"

Bang!

After Adda Krispus pointed that dainty pistol at John's head and ended his life, the whole room began to spin. My vision went white, brilliant white, and didn't return to normal until I heard Tony Basillio shouting at me.

"Get help, Swede! Call the cops! Hurry!" He was stooping near John's fallen body and his trousers were stained red at the knee.

I headed for the door, but stopped in my tracks, afraid. Even though the gun was lying on John's chest, not in Adda's hands, I was afraid somehow she might shoot me in the back as I ran. Afraid that she would kill Basillio while I was getting the police. Afraid she'd jump out of the nearest window. Just afraid.

It was as though the murderess knew what I was thinking. "There's no need to hurry," Adda Krispus had said, an edge of annoyance in her voice. "Just go and get them. The both of you. Just go ahead and get out."

Tony and I exchanged stunned, confused glances. He got to his feet, and together we backed out of the apartment and scrambled down the stairs to the nearest phone.

It was all noise and chaos after that.

Ambulance. Screeching patrol cars. Shocked neighbors. Even a stray reporter.

And now here we were on the set of *Naked City*.

I didn't care how indecorous it looked—I unbuttoned my blouse nearly down to the navel.

Basillio was reaching for my hand again.

"Miss Alice Nestleton?"

A solid, light-haired man of medium height was calling my name.

"I'm Stoner." He proffered his hand.

I took mine out of my pocket and shook hands with him.

"And you're Basillio, right?" He looked down at Tony, who was still seated.

"Yeah," was Tony's only answer. And he kept his seat.

"All right," Stoner said. "We should be able to let you two get home soon. I just want to go over a couple of things again before I wrap up the report." He hesitated for a minute then, looking first at Tony and then at me. "Let's see . . . Miss Nestleton, how about you first?"

Inside Lieutenant Stoner's office I confirmed—or reconfirmed—the details of the shooting of John Cerise.

He listened intently to my summary, not moving a muscle, barely taking a breath. It was rare to see that kind of concentration. I was reminded of the dozens of times I'd heard acting teachers shouting, remonstrating, shrieking at students: You're not listening! You're not listening! You must learn to listen!

After I finished with the facts, he switched over into a slightly different mode of questioning.

"How well did you know the victim? Did you see much of him? Did the two of you talk often?"

The "victim." I hated the sound of that. I didn't want John to be called "the victim"— even if that was exactly what he was.

"I've known John Cerise for years, Lieutenant," I said. "I spoke to him periodically—regularly—but not what you'd call often. I actually saw him even less than that. Once, perhaps twice a year. But I still thought of him as my friend."

"Any idea why Adda Krispus would want to kill him?"

"No, no. I don't know why anyone would want to kill John. But then of course I don't know Adda Krispus."

"It says here in the report that you and Mr. . . . Mr. . . . ." He leafed through the papers in the folder in front of him.

"Basillio?" I supplied.

"Right. The report says you definitely recognized the victim and Mr. Basillio thought he did, too, but Cerise denied he was Cerise. Is that true?"

"Yes, it is."

"Tell me exactly what he said, if you can remember."

"Well, he stepped out of the bathroom and looked at us. When I saw who it was, I said something like, John, what are you doing here? and he said, My name isn't John. Twice, he said it. Just like that: My name isn't John."

"So you think the Krispus couple knew him under some other name."

"I have no idea."

"Any idea why he would deny being John Cerise?"

"No, Lieutenant," I said sternly, "I don't."

Little by little the haze of confusion and

bewilderment was leaving me and anger was taking its place. I think I may have been tapping my toe against my side of the desk.

"We'll be finished here in just a bit," Stoner said, reading me just right. "Can I get you some coffee?"

"All right. Sure."

I thought he was going to leave the room in search of a vending machine, giving me a few minutes alone with my own thoughts. But no. He didn't have to go anywhere. Right there on the sill of a boarded-up window was a Mr. Coffee contraption half filled with a rank-looking liquid.

"Sugar?" Lieutenant Stoner asked.

"Yes, several."

I watched him while he pulled open drawers in search of sugar packets and plastic stirrers. As he moved about, the ringlets of moisture at each armpit seemed to spread. Or was that an optical illusion?

He was wearing an old-fashioned summer white shirt with the sleeves rolled up—perhaps it was an Arrow, the brand favored by the bank teller in the town near the farm where I grew up. Yes, Arrow Shirts—how well I remember their colorful ads—I wondered if the company still existed.

Stoner must have been about fifty, an age

that would have entitled him to a bit of a potbelly. But he didn't have one.

I took a sip of the thick coffee.

True to his word, he kept me only fifteen minutes more. He had one final question: "When Adda Krispus shouted Look! and then pointed the gun at your friend John, why didn't you and Mr. Basillio do something?"

"*Do* something?" I repeated. "Like tackle her?"

"Not necessarily. What about screaming? What about trying to talk her out of it?"

"I don't think you understand how quickly things happened in that room, Lieutenant. We were—I was disoriented. It was so . . . so . . . crazy . . . I thought maybe even it was a joke. That the gun wasn't real. That John was going to break into laughter. That all the other guests were suddenly going to pop out from behind the curtains and yell Surprise or something. It's just not the kind of thing you're prepared for."

"Sure. I understand. You probably haven't ever had to deal with that kind of violence."

"Well, I wouldn't say that—not exactly."

He waited for me to go on, but I made an on-the-spot decision not to elaborate. I'd learned from some pretty unpleasant past experiences that it wasn't always a good idea to tell a cop that you're in the business of solving crimes yourself.

"You look pretty tired," Lieutenant Stoner said solicitously.

"That's not exactly true either. I'm exhausted."

"Okay. You can go now."

I got to my feet. I must have moved too quickly, because suddenly my head felt as light as a soap bubble.

Stoner stepped around the desk and took my arm. "I can get somebody to give you a lift home. Or find you a cab. It's late."

"Thanks, but I think I'll wait for Tony—Mr. Basillio, I mean. I don't suppose you know a place where I could get something to eat at this hour?"

"Sure I do. Where are we—Minnesota? The city never sleeps."

I didn't laugh. Nor did I explain that I don't take kindly to people slurring Minnesota, my home, as a backwash where the lights go out at nine o'clock.

"Just up the block," Stoner went on, "there's a place. Pal Joey, it's called. Food's good. You could get something to eat and wait for your friend there. You'll like it. It's safe."

"Why? Do all the policemen eat there?"

"Not on their salaries."

"Oh? And what are you—an eccentric millionaire who does this for fun?"

"Nope. I'm a wage slave, too. But food isn't something I economize on. I was born in New Orleans."

He said that as if it explained everything. Well, perhaps it did. I'd never met anybody from New Orleans who didn't prize a good meal above just about all else.

The phone rang. The lieutenant picked it up and listened with that same concentration for a minute or so. Then he walked me out to the desk, where Basillio was cooling himself in front of the fan.

"What's happening now?" Tony asked warily.

"It's okay—" I began, but Stoner spoke at the same moment.

"It's okay," he echoed. "This won't take long, Cap."

Cap? Why did he call Tony "Cap"? Basillio's double take said that he was wondering the same thing.

"There's a place up the street, Tony," I said. "A restaurant called . . ."

"Pal Joey," said the lieutenant.

"Cute," Basillio mumbled.

"Tony, I'll go mad if I don't get a drink and something to eat. I thought I'd wait there for you."

"All right. I'll see you there as soon as the beating is over." He turned toward Stoner and smirked.

The lieutenant returned the look, but then added: "Actually, this thing is all but wrapped up. Seems the shooter's already confessed."

"Not a hell of a lot else she could do," Tony snapped. "We saw it all."

"Right," Lieutenant Stoner said. "I guess she figured that one out. She says she did it and she's not particularly sorry."

"But why?" I cried.

"That, the lady will not tell. Even when we said 'please.' "

"She must be crazy," Basillio said.

"Maybe," Stoner said quietly.

I said nothing.

I watched the two of them go into the office and close the door behind them.

The bar looked very inviting through the window.

I glanced quickly at the hand-lettered menu posted next to the door. PAL JOEY BISTRO was spelled out in burgundy ink.

Steak *frites*. Grilled salmon. Onion soup. Goat cheese this. Sautéed that.

It sounded right.

True, it was a sultry summer night. True, the garden salad as described on the menu sounded lovely. True, meat might sit rather heavily on the stomach on such a night. But that is what I craved: meat, and plenty of it. I was starving.

I walked directly to the bar and ordered red wine. A bottle. After all, I was expecting Tony.

The bartender smiled and placed a menu in front of me when I asked if the kitchen was still open.

I hadn't paid a great deal of attention to the prices listed on the menu outside. Now I could get a good look. An incredible $10.95 for a hamburger with french fries! An outrage.

But I was so hungry I would have paid double.

I told the bartender I'd start with a tomato salad, followed by the goat cheese and onion tart, and then go on to the hamburger—rare.

I looked at my watch. It was 1:49. Someone had told me that in Barcelona, dinner at midnight was nothing out of the ordinary.

As distraught as I was, I couldn't help laughing to myself.

Lieutenant Stoner hadn't lied. The tart was excellent. I took my fork and hunted down every crumb on the plate.

I was methodically working my way to the middle of the wine bottle.

The potatoes were placed before me first. Shoestring thin. Piping hot. I drank in the aroma, popping a couple of them into my mouth even as I picked up the salt shaker.

And then the burger arrived.

Looking like a stray hunk of cement from a construction site. And just as hard.

That did it!

I'd been holding back a torrent of rage all night, ever since the moment Adda Krispus raised that gun. I could hold it back no longer.

I began to screech in the most unattractive way imaginable.

When the sweet-faced young bartender walked hurriedly back to me, it was all I could do not to grasp the collar of his white shirt and shake him. "How dare you serve something like this?" I cawed at him.

"Like what, ma'am?"

"This charred brick!"

I pushed the plate violently toward the far

side of the bar. "You people have a lot of nerve asking eleven dollars for something like this!"

My voice had risen to uncontrollable heights.

I knew it was more than the overdone meat I was upset about. I'd been through the mill—several mills—more mills than anybody should have to endure on a hot night in New York City. Above all, my friend John was dead. And I had had to witness it.

Every eye in the restaurant was on me, but I paid the other customers—and there was something of a crowd for two in the morning—no mind whatsoever.

Oh, how I carried on.

"You people are no better than criminals, and I refuse to pay for this garbage!" I shouted. "I absolutely, unconditionally refuse! And tell the manager I want to see him right away."

"I'll just do that right now, ma'am."

"Yes," I said tauntingly as he retreated. "You just do that little thing. You get the manager, or whoever's in charge in this pretentious little . . . *bistro*."

I downed another glass of bordeaux. I was too angry to cry.

"Who in hell is keeping up that racket?" came from the rear of the dining room.

I saw the bartender point me out to the sturdy-looking red-haired woman in a chef's apron.

She took a long look at me and then began thundering toward me like a buffalo in heat.

"Now you see here, Missy," the woman blustered, "if you can't keep a civil tongue in your head, I'll kick you right out of . . . Oh my God . . . *Alice?!*"

At the sound of my own name, I sat bolt upright on the plush barstool. This woman knew me! Lord, what kind of turn would the evening take now?

"Alice . . . it is you, isn't it?"

"Nora? I can't believe it! Nora?"

"Yes!"

She rushed up to the bar and we embraced like long lost friends—which is precisely what we were.

I sat on a high stool in the kitchen, trying to explain all that had happened earlier that night, while Nora made me steak Diane. It turned out my hamburger order had been confused with someone else's.

Nora Karroll, born Norma Jones, changed

her name in the 1960s, not only because she thought the new name would sound more glamorous on a theater marquee but because she feared if she kept her own name she'd be confused with Shirley Jones, the actress who was getting all the musical roles Nora felt should have gone to her in the first place.

By the time Tony and I met Nora at the Dramatic Workshop, in the '70s, the Broadway musical had changed drastically, almost disappeared in fact, and Nora, a good ten years older than most of us, was going after dramatic parts.

We had never been tremendously close, but she had been awfully sweet and helpful to me. And on more than a few occasions she had asked a group of us poor students over for dinner. She was some cook—even then.

She hadn't worked as an actress in years, she said. She and her late husband had lived in Europe for five years and while she was there she studied with a respected chef. When she got back to New York, she decided to open her own place. Good food—basic stuff with a French flair.

"I don't get so much work anymore myself," I told her. "I had to develop a new way to make a living, too."

"No kidding? What?"

"I sit for cats."

"You what?"

"I take care of cats. You know, someone's away for a week. I go over to the apartment, feed the cat, play with him or her, change the cat box, take them to the vet. Maybe I water the plants, wait for packages to be delivered. You know."

"Alice, you're still a nut."

It surprised me to hear her say that. "Am I? I never thought of myself as a nut."

"Of course not. That's why you're a nut. You used to read a script and say the craziest crap in the world about it, or about your character. And you'd say it with an absolutely straight face. Like it was normal. You believed it. And so nobody else questioned it. Pretty soon it started to seem normal to everybody else, too."

"How strange," I said. "I always thought of myself as utterly normal—dull even. Well, sometimes."

"What else are you up to?"

I hesitated with my answer.

"What's the matter? Doing something you're embarrassed about?"

"You're *really* going to think this is strange, Nora."

"Try me."

"I sometimes . . . how do I say it? . . . check things out for people—sort of private investigator work. Often for people with cats. And occasionally I solve murders."

"See what I mean, Alice?" She picked up my plate and led me back out to the dining room. "See?"

I gave Nora the short version of my marriage and divorce. She gave me the comic version of her year on a TV soap opera, the only work she could find as an actress back in the late '70s. They wrote her out of the script by having her character, Mrs. Hufnagle, burn to death in a beauty shop fire.

It was so good—and so weird—to be laughing that way, reminiscing with one old friend, when another had just been murdered.

"I was completely lost in those days," Nora said dreamily. "I didn't know what was going to become of me. You kids were all so young and talented and you welcomed me into your crowd. And all the teachers were so inspiring. Do you see much of the old crowd?"

"No, not very much. Except for Tony, of course."

"Which one? Tony Allen? You and he had a thing, didn't you?"

"No. Basillio."

"Oh, *that* Tony! My goodness, it's been an age since I saw him, too. Remember that wild set he did for *Lady Windemere*? He's married with kids, isn't he?"

"He was."

"Uh-huh. And the two of you—"

"Yes. Off and on. Forever off and on. He's helped me on some of my cases."

"Is that what he was doing tonight, when your friend was shot?"

"No. The other way around, almost. I'd never have been there if Tony hadn't dragged me to what was supposed to be a fund-raiser for that ridiculous Peter Krispus."

The restaurant door opened just then.

"Well, speak of the devil!" Nora exclaimed. "Here's our gorgeous Harvey Keitel right now!"

I snapped to attention. "What? Where?"

It was Basillio.

Nora flew over to him, arms open.

The two of them were lost in a blizzard of "I don't believe it!" and "You look great!"

Watching them chatter, I had a thought I had not had in a long time: God, anything can happen in New York.

Chapter 3

It was light outside by the time Tony and I got to bed.

I had an awful night. Well, you could hardly call it "night." In and out of bed half a dozen times. Tossing and turning. Bad dreams.

Tony slept like a zombie, body curled tightly in upon itself. I had to wonder what kind of dreams were going on behind his eyes.

I got out of bed around one in the afternoon. I put water on to boil.

Tony woke up a few minutes later, looking crushed and rumpled—about like I felt.

"Good morning," he said wryly, stretching.

I set his cup of coffee down on the nightstand and walked away without saying a word.

"What—no bacon and eggs?" he said playfully.

"They're in the Cuisinart," I answered, deadpan.

He ran his tongue over his teeth and took a few swallows of coffee. Then he threw back the sheet and swung his legs over the side of the bed.

The sight of him walking naked toward the bathroom jarred me. I turned my back.

As soon as he went in, a loud cat cry went up. Bushy came zooming out, looking all frazzled and flustered. That prompted Pancho to get in on the act. He wailed stupidly from his hideaway on top of the refrigerator.

"Quiet down, you two!" I commanded. "I mean it!"

I could hear Tony rummaging in the medicine cabinet; toilet flushing; water running; brushing of teeth.

Each sound seemed to go right through me. Like fingernails across a blackboard. Like banging your funny bone. Like the dripping faucet in the middle of the night.

Tony padded leisurely through the kitchen, where I sat slicing oranges. Again I averted my eyes. I didn't know why his nakedness grated on me so much. It just did.

He went back over to the bed and picked up his cup, and then he pushed the curtain aside and stood there drinking coffee and looking out at the day.

"Looks like another hot one, Swede," he said.

"Yes—Tony, for god's sake will you put some clothes on!"

He turned, startled, and let the curtain fall back into place.

"What? Oh . . . okay."

After he was dressed he walked over to me and held out his cup. "Is the second one still free of charge?"

"Sure," I said, and set about making more.

Tony went over to the refrigerator. "I guess the bacon and eggs are really a fantasy, huh?" he asked.

"If you find them, you can make them," I said.

"Well, never mind. I see the bouncer is guarding the door to the fridge, anyway."

He meant Pancho, who was still up there, baring his teeth now.

"Yeah, I love you, too, cat," he muttered.

He took a seat next to me then and bit into one of the orange quarters.

"That was really something, seeing Nora like that, wasn't it?" he said, grinning.

"Yes, it was."

"You don't seem too happy about—"

"*Excuse* me, Tony," I interrupted him—I knew how filthy my tone was. "Our little reunion with Nora was very, very nice. But it is *not* the first thing on my mind this morning. We just saw a friend of mine get shot in the head, if you recall."

He seemed to collapse then, like a tire with a nail in it.

"Sure, I remember," he said quietly. "I'm sorry. How are you about that?"

He reached for me then, being sympathetic, being sensitive, just being human.

I knew it would be unspeakably mean of me to pull away from him, and so I didn't. Although I wanted to.

I tried responding to his question. "I'm . . . I guess I'm . . ."

God, I didn't know how to finish that sentence. I didn't know how to characterize how I was "about that."

And so I just shook my head and lifted myself out of the chair, getting busy with yet another cup of instant espresso.

We breakfasted on whatever we could find in the cabinets—bread, jam, year-old Rice

Krispies. Actually, Tony ate alone. I didn't feel like eating, not even an orange.

Bushy had taken it upon himself to occupy the third seat at the table, hoping, no doubt, for a chance at the leftover milk at the bottom of Basillio's cereal bowl.

As usual, Tony kept up an inane one-way conversation with the cat, the gist of which was how foppish and spoiled Bushy was.

When Bushy finally made his move—lunging at the bowl—Tony plucked it away just in time. And then he dipped his finger into the milk and flicked a few beads of it at poor, frustrated Bushy. Who then resumed his earpiercing caterwauling.

That tore it.

I turned on Basillio like a cornered lioness.

I can't even remember most of the names I called him. But half of them I hadn't uttered since my first boyfriend—we were nine years old—taught me how to cuss.

My anger was like a mighty river: age-old, raging, unstoppable, fearsome. All those feelings I didn't know what to do with? I had converted them to acid. And now I was bathing Tony in it. Scalding him. Deforming him.

It was an easy transition for me to make— from blessing Tony out for his treatment of

Bushy to blaming him for what had happened yesterday. I was in such a state that the two things had become of a piece.

"You persist in some goddamn phony nostalgia about Peter Goddamn Krispus and his contribution to the *theater!*" I screamed at him. "He's one of *us,* you claim. One of us! When you probably never even set eyes on one of his stupid, self-indulgent operas!

"And then you can't even get the date right for his ridiculous charity rent party. You drag me over to that stinking old tenement in this miserable soggy weather . . . only to make me watch my friend John being blown to bits.

"My God, man! If you hadn't finished that bottle of wine before we left . . . if your mind weren't so . . . so . . . if you weren't such a posturing juvenile . . . We just never would have been there, that's all!

"In fact, there might not have been a murder at all if we hadn't been there!

"And now, John is . . . John is dead. Dead, Basillio!"

Tony looked as if he wanted to throttle me as badly as I wanted to throttle him. But he waited a few seconds before speaking.

"Are you finished?" he asked, his voice ropy and dark.

"No!"

"No, Alice? No? You mean there's more of this crap? What are you going to blame me for now—killing Lincoln?"

"That's very funny, Tony. But you know very well what I'm saying. John might be alive today if we hadn't gone there last night."

"That is the most ridiculous thing you have ever said in your life—which is saying a lot, my friend!"

"At this moment I am definitely not your friend, Tony. Not, not, not! But I am going to tell you why I said what I did, and I don't care if you think it's crap.

"I think that John might still be alive today because that woman Adda Krispus was waiting for witnesses to what she was going to do. If we hadn't been there to see it, she might not have pulled that trigger."

"That's not only crap, Alice, it's crazy crap! Adda didn't even know who we were. She'd never even met you before."

"That is irrelevant to the point," I insisted. "I believe she needed someone to watch her kill John. And we were there to oblige her. She saw the opportunity and took it.

"And why were we there, Tony? Why were *you* there? Why are you there every year? To help that pathetic old man pay the rent? No! Certainly not. You go there so you can prey on a new set of impressionable young actresses. Girls young enough to be your daughters. Girls who're still naive enough to think you're Mr. Theater. Mr. Out-of-Work Integrity. Mr. Cool. Mr. I've worked with the great ones. Mr. I *am* one of the great ones even if nobody knows it. In a word, Tony, you were hoping to score!"

His mouth contorted in a way that made me want to rip his lips off.

"Is that what this nonsense is about, Swede? Jealousy? You think I want to leave you for somebody younger!"

I didn't think it was possible to be any madder than I was up to that point, but I was wrong.

I shrieked at him: "Don't flatter yourself, Tony!" And when I laughed, it sounded like something from hell. "But telling you that is rather like telling a duck not to quack, isn't it? Jealous? Was I jealous when you spent the night with Annie Dean, my agent's new secretary?"

He went white.

"Don't bother trying to think of a comeback, Basillio. Don't tax your brain. Yes, I knew about it. Just as I know you don't sleep alone when you get jobs for the summer. No. You hold court in the bar after the show. And then, when you've had a few belts, you help yourself to all the young flesh you can get your mitts on. And then you come back to the city—back to me— mewling that I don't love you . . . or love you enough . . . or love you in the right way.

"It's an old old scene by now. A scene from an old warhorse of a play, Basillio. And frankly I am bored to death by it."

Tony's eyes filled with an awful blackness then.

"So," he said calmly, "the lady is bored. Well, that is the capital crime in Nestleton-land, isn't it? In that faraway land of make-believe. That land where nobody else can go, because it's all in your head.

"Goodness! Mustn't bore Alice. She'll go a long way not to be bored. Even so far as to make up an insane scenario to explain the tragedy of her friend's death. Yes, anything to keep Lady Nestleton amused."

"Amused! You think John's death amuses me? Do you know how horribly you've insulted me, Basillio?"

"Yes," he said simply.

Suddenly he was standing. Looking down at me.

There was a cold lump in my chest. "Where are you going, Tony?"

"I'm out, Alice."

"What does that mean—out?"

"Out means . . . out. Out of here, out of your old place . . . out of your life. And you're out of mine, lady. It's over."

"Tony!" I called threateningly.

"I'll mail you the keys when I find a new place," he said.

And he was out the door.

Tony had left a white undershirt behind. I grabbed it from the foot of the bed and threw it into the trash.

I drank enough espresso to power a small plane. It didn't help. My body felt heavy. My brain, too.

I put off the postmortem on the argument for as long as I could. I tried to tell myself a breakup is a breakup is a breakup. I was a big girl and I'd broken up with men before.

And then the recriminations came. And the anger was renewed.

I couldn't stop that merry-go-round of emotions: Desolate. Sorry. Enraged. Sorry. Justified. Insulted. Sorry. Guilty. Sorry. Alone. Defiant. Sorry.

The cats came and went from my lap. The songs came and went on the radio. The afternoon shadows lengthened.

Finally, I got up and retrieved Tony's shirt. And sat holding it in my lap while I cried.

Chapter 4

I fed the cats an early dinner. As soon as they saw me rummaging in the cabinet, they gathered around me. I wasn't paying much attention to what kind of can I opened. For all I knew, I was feeding them kitty salmon for the third day in a row. But they didn't complain. I didn't even keep up the usual line of dinnertime patter with them that they seemed to look forward to.

Then I changed into some tan linen trousers and a T-shirt and sandals.

I had nowhere to go, really, but I just knew I had to get out of the house.

There wasn't very much to be happy about. But at least it was cocktail hour.

I walked up Hudson Street until it began to transmute into 8th Avenue. Only when I passed 23rd Street did I know for sure where I was going.

I needed to talk to Nora.

I continued walking uptown.

Business was good. The bar was crowded.

The young man I had bawled out the other night gave me a cautious nod in greeting.

Nora was sitting alone at a booth near the front of the dining room, adding up receipts on a pocket calculator.

"Well, hello, Alice. Looks like you might become a regular here. I'm thrilled."

"Don't be too thrilled," I warned her. "I'm here to cry on your shoulder a little."

"That's okay. Goes along with the territory. What's wrong?"

"I just broke up with Tony. Again. I mean, for good . . . I guess."

"What did he do this time?"

"It's hard to explain. Besides, I don't know if it was *all* his fault. We started talking about what happened at Krispus's place and I said some things and he said some things and before I knew it, we were screaming at each other and he walked out."

"He'll be back."

"I don't know. This time, I don't know. Anyway, John's death has got me just as crazy as the fight with Tony. I just haven't accepted that he's dead—not that he died in that way, at least. It was all so stupid."

Nora signaled to the young bartender, who hopped to it and arrived at the table in nothing flat.

"What are you drinking, Alice?" she said.

"Nothing in particular. I don't know. Whatever."

"Oh, you are depressed, aren't you honey?" she said pityingly. "Gregg, make my friend Alice a nice Negroni."

I calmed down with the second Negroni, which I'd never tasted nor heard of before that day, but which turned out to be Campari mixed with gin and sweet vermouth. It really is quite delicious.

And by then I had explained to Nora how I met John Cerise and the unique character of our friendship—"almost like a correspondence by mail," I described it. "I almost never saw him. But he was such a lovely person. I just can't believe he would be involved with a group of people—any group of people—using a false name. It all sounds so sinister, so underhanded. And that wasn't John at all. He never for a moment acted like a person with something to hide.

"Not that I knew very much about him. I can't even call his family to say how sorry I am. I don't know if he had any family. It's so frustrating."

"Well, he's gone now, hon. That crazy woman isn't telling why she shot him. And there isn't a thing you can do to make her tell. You may never know the real story."

"I know, I know. That's what makes me so . . . so . . . mad."

"And curious?"

"Yes, that, too."

"What are you going to do, Alice?" she asked, suddenly suspicious.

"What makes you think I'm going to do anything?"

She waved off my question. "Oh, you're planning to do something. I can tell."

"Maybe. But what? I'm not sure where to start."

"Oh, come on. Just go into your private dick number. Get in character. What would Sam Spade do?"

I shrugged, beginning to be depressed all over again. "Have another drink?" I asked flippantly.

Nora laughed. "What about having dinner with me here tonight? I'm expecting a pal to join me. It'll be fun."

"You're being so nice, Nora. I don't know if I can eat anything right now."

"Not now. Later. After you start the investigation."

I looked at her for a long moment.

"Yes," I said at last. "I suppose I am going to start an investigation of some kind. It's driving me crazy not knowing why John died."

"Good. A hard shift of detecting work ought to put you in the mood for tonight's specialty."

"Which is . . . ?"

"Cassoulet."

"I've heard of it but never tried it."

"Oh, boy, you've got an experience ahead of you. It's lousy with sausage and duck fat and everything else that stops your heart—and it's full of beans—if you know what I mean."

"You're on, Nora. I'd be happy to dine with you."

"You can walk there from here, right?"

"Walk where?" I asked, puzzled.

"To Krispus's place," she said. "The scene of the crime, as they say on the *Late Show*."

Of course. I was so sad and confused that all my senses had been blunted. My instincts seemed to have deserted me.

Of course! I had to go back to that damn old tenement apartment.

For a moment I felt acute embarrassment that Nora seemed to be choreographing my moves. But wasn't I begging for just that kind of help?

Maybe I'd find nothing there. But at least, with Adda Krispus behind bars, another killing was unlikely.

"Don't take any wooden nickels, Sam," Nora called to me as I picked up my purse and headed for the front door.

The last time I saw Peter Krispus he was lying still on his high bed, breathing shallowly, oblivious, it seemed, to the fact that someone had just been shot to death in his living room.

So I didn't know what to expect when the door to the Krispus's bleak railroad flat swung open.

Certainly not the well-groomed brunette in a tailored, powder blue suit—no doubt a good thrift shop purchase—who stood before me, serene blue eyes looking into mine.

"Hello," I said tentatively. "This is the Peter Krispus residence, isn't it?"

"Yes."

She waited silently for me to go on.

"Hello. I'm Alice Nestleton. I was—unfortunately, I was here the evening your—Mrs. Krispus, that is—was arrested for the shooting of John Cerise."

She continued to gaze at me. So long that I thought perhaps she was blind.

I wished mightily, right then, that Tony were beside me.

"Oh," she said finally.

That's all. Just Oh.

"Was Mrs. Krispus—I mean, *is* Mrs. Krispus—your mother?"

"No. Adda's my mother-in-law. Or was. You were more right than wrong to put it in the past tense, I suspect."

I heard voices from deep inside the apartment. The young woman was a hair shorter than I. I tried to look past her shoulder into the flat.

"I don't mean to intrude, Mrs. Krispus," I said, "but I was wondering if I could come in for a minute."

Before she could answer, a male voice called, "Jane, who is that?"

Her eyes did not leave mine. She did not answer the question that had been posed.

"Please . . ." she said, opening the door wider and allowing me to step in. "I'm very sorry, I didn't recognize your name at first."

Standing together in the room where John died were two middle-aged men, both holding highball glasses. One was quite tall and rawboned with sandy hair; he was dressed

in chinos and a blousy short-sleeve shirt.
The other man, a softer, shorter, and slightly older version of him, wore a dark suit that
was plainly cut from fine material, but far
past its prime.

"This is Alice Nestleton," the woman announced to the two men, who watched me
approach. "Miss Nestleton, this is my husband Hume."

The rangy one applied the same kind of
placid glance to my face. He nodded hello.

"And this," Jane Krispus said, "is my
brother-in-law, Merlin."

The shorter man shook my hand and
murmured "how do you do?"

I addressed them as a group. "First of all,
I wanted to say how sorry I am this whole
thing happened. And sorry if I'm disturbing
you all. I know this can't be a good time for
you. But I was here last night—"

"Yes, I know," Merlin Krispus cut me off.
"The police told us everything. And we want
to express our sympathies to you, over the
loss of your friend."

"Thanks. I'll come to the point quickly. I
was hoping you could tell me something
more about John—maybe help me locate his
family."

Three sets of blank, uncomprehending

eyes were trained on me. At that very moment, I realized that the cats were nowhere in sight. Where were they? I wondered.

"I don't understand," Merlin said slowly. "Wasn't he your friend?"

"Yes," I said. "But I knew little about his past or where he came from. I thought since he was a family friend of yours, you could tell me."

"Of ours? No." It was Hume who spoke. "Presumably he was one of my father's many acquaintances. But none of the rest of us ever met Mr. Cerise."

"Really?" I said. "I was under the impression your parents knew him fairly well, but perhaps under some other name than John Cerise. I assumed you knew him, too."

"Not at all," Jane said. "By the way, can I make you a drink?"

"Thank you, no."

Well, that was a disappointment.

I looked around the tatty room then, random images from the night of the murder popping in and out of my head.

I shook those thoughts away as best I could.

"I don't suppose your father could be of help?" I asked.

"Not likely," Hume answered grimly.

"No. Not likely at all," Merlin said as he stepped over to refill his glass from the long-necked bottle of J&B that stood alone on the mantel. "Father's not even sure where he is most of the time. Frankly, Miss Nestleton, it's touch and go with my father. He is in very frail health and we just don't know how long he has."

"I see."

What I didn't see was the elder Mr. Krispus. I looked down the hallway, toward the outer room. It would be hard to miss that cold steel bed on its big rubber wheels.

"Ah!"

There was another voice in the room now. The only voice I'd ever heard in that house with any semblance of liveliness or cheer in it.

A short, slightly stooped man was looking me over with open sexual interest. His graying hair was greasy and windblown and he wore a gauzy Indian shirt over soiled gray pants.

"Ah!" he repeated. "And who is this enchanting visitor?"

Hume Krispus glanced at the old gentleman in distaste. Then he turned away and lit a cigarette.

I couldn't much blame him. The old man

looked a little like Barrymore in makeup as Svengali.

"Miss Nestleton, this is Luther Kaminecki," Jane said. "Luther is Peter's colleague of many years—and his biographer."

Mr. Kaminecki took my hand in both of his and turned it palm up, as if to study it. "Charmed, Miss Nestleton. Charmed. An actress, yes?"

It took me aback. "Why, yes."

"Of course you are." He seemed extremely pleased with himself.

"Miss Nestleton was a friend of John Cerise," Jane explained. "She thought we might have known him."

"A friend of John . . . ?" he asked.

"Cerise," Hume said crisply, enunciating carefully. "Mother killed him, Luther—remember?"

Slowly I extracted my hand from Luther's grasp.

Brother Merlin smiled a bit indulgently, and a bit falsely, at Mr. Kaminecki. "How is Father, Luther?"

"He is almost asleep," the old man said gently.

A silence fell over the room.

"Well, I think I should probably be going now," I announced. "But before I do, would it be possible—I mean, might I just look in on your father—to pay my respects?"

They all exchanged glances, all of them unreadable.

Then, in a minute, Merlin said, "Of course. That's very thoughtful of you. Come this way."

I followed him down the narrow hallway.

We reached a musty room covered from ceiling to floor with posters, framed newspaper clippings, pen-and-ink drawings, sheet music, and the like.

A harrowingly thin nurse of about sixty was tidying the papers on a clunky, chipped desk. She did not speak to us.

There was Peter Krispus on his death chariot. Still. Breathing in and out. Above it all. The bed had been moved so it was no longer visible from the hallway.

And at the foot of the bed, like two palace guards, sat the mighty Maine coons, their eyes following our every move.

Merlin drew close to his father. "I'm afraid he is asleep now," he said.

"Yes," I answered. "I can see that he is."

The two silver beasts continued to watch me, as if daring me to step any closer.

I couldn't make out the details of the riot of artwork and memorabilia on the walls.

Too bad. They might have provided more insight into Peter Krispus—and maybe John Cerise—than any of the people in this apartment had been able to do.

Just who were all these people, who seemed like characters in a second level Daphne DuMaurier novel? Shabby but well-spoken, articulate, educated. Poor but refined.

And all of them hiding something. All of them liars.

Now, why did I think that?

I couldn't put my finger on it, but there was something about their manner that made me suspect that each and every one of them knew perfectly well who John Cerise was.

When I left the apartment I took the stairs two at a time.

Out on the street again, I felt a lot better. That apartment had grown suffocating with the evening fug.

Maybe it was nothing more than the enervating wet heat that had given me those suspicions about the Krispus clan.

The older I got, the more brutal the New York summers seemed. My niece's lover had already provided me with a nice apartment.

Perhaps someday he'd give me a summer home as well.

Dream on, girl.

I looked forward to the air-conditioning in Nora's bistro. I had another night of heavy food ahead of me.

Chapter 5

The things they do in the name of progress! It makes me want to spit sometimes.

Everybody and his uncle with a product to sell can now call you in your home, anytime, day or night, and try to sell you something over the phone.

As a person with unconventional hours, I'm at home in my loft a good part of the day. Hardly a day passes when I don't get one of those damn calls—wouldn't you like to have the *Times* delivered, Miss Nestleton? Wouldn't you like to invest in junk bonds? How about plastic surgery? New Age light-bulbs? A condominium in Jakarta?

The phone rang about ten in the morning, a couple of days after my encounter with the Krispus clan. The voice on the other end of the line, a woman's voice, began to talk nonstop as soon as I said hello. When they don't give you a chance to say anything, it's a sure sign that it's one of those hateful calls.

This one, apparently, was a charity—something about a refuge for feral cats. Well, somebody *really* had my number, didn't they?

I was just about to hang up when I heard the phrase "alley cats."

I listened a little more closely then.

The lady on the other end, a Miss Glenda Fuchs, was the chairman of a group called OAC—Our Alley Cats. Would I consider making a donation to this worthy organization, which was dedicated to the rescue of homeless kitties, who would be sheltered and fed and neutered in the OAC facility on Long Island?

I wrote down the address and agreed to send a check.

"Oh, thank you, Miss Nestleton," she said. "Every penny helps. But actually, there was something else I wanted to talk to you about. It's the real purpose of my call."

The *real* purpose. I didn't like the sound of that. What was coming next? Was I expected to volunteer my time, too? Or turn over my savings account to these people? Or put on a sari and beg for money in airports?

"What else?" I asked cautiously.

"Actually, it's another plea for a little contribution. I'm trying to raise enough money to bury John Cerise."

The sound of his name sat me up straight. "What did you say?" I asked, stunned.

"John Cerise," she repeated carefully, then added, "Oh, dear . . . you *were* aware that he died?"

"Yes, to be sure. But how . . . I mean, was John a friend of yours?"

"A colleague, really. He worked with us at OAC. He was a board member, as a matter of fact. But he was such a nice man, it was easy to think of him as a friend rather than just a coworker. I was so saddened to hear he was dead. And in that shocking way— murdered!

"You see, no one has come forward to claim his body. And I can't just let them bury him in potter's field. I'd like to have a proper service for him when the coroner releases his body—and maybe order a special marker for the grave . . . Or perhaps cremation would be better. I don't know. I just thought maybe you'd have some idea what he'd want done.

"He mentioned your name from time to

time, quite fondly. And you were on his mailing list for our next fund-raising drive."

"I see," I said solemnly. "Well, you can count on me to help with John's burial."

The line went quiet for a few seconds. I wondered whether Miss Fuchs had suddenly choked up, as I had, thinking about John's senseless killing, and the loss of him.

"Let me ask," I said a moment later, "if you have spoken to any of his neighbors. Perhaps they knew something about his family."

"Neighbors?"

"Yes, out in New Jersey. He had a home there."

"Oh, that. No. He sold the house a while ago. He'd been living in Manhattan for nearly a year. He was subletting a place on the Upper West Side."

That was surprising. I was still imagining John rambling around in his huge house, being followed from one room to the other by his cats.

When I said as much to Miss Fuchs, she sighed. "Yes, I can imagine the same scene," she said. "But John was so devoted to his brood, when the last of the old cats died, he said he didn't want to have any new ones for a while. I don't think he had any animals in the apartment."

"Where was the apartment?" I asked.

"Let me see," she replied thoughtfully. "West End Avenue, I believe. In the nineties. Ninety-fifth perhaps? No, Ninety-second, I think. I believe I dropped him there once in a taxi."

We talked a few minutes more and then Miss Fuchs said she had to get back to her calls.

I said I appreciated her contacting me, and I assured her I would do what I could to help her. Help her with both of her worthy causes.

Bushy jumped up on the kitchen table just about then. Though admittedly he is an egomaniac, that cat is one of the most simpatico creatures I've ever known—intuitive. Worried about me, he looked into my eyes and mewed a few words of sympathy. I chastised him halfheartedly when he began to poke his nose into my coffee cup. I plucked him off the tabletop and deposited him on the chair next to mine.

Life goes on, as they say. I went into my bag and searched for my checkbook. I really did want to help the cat rescue program, OAC.

But the minute I wrote out the check, it occurred to me that I was being a bit over-generous. This was no time, financially speaking, for me to make a grand gesture: Tony Basillio was moving out of my old 26th Street place. It meant that the rent there was once again my responsibility, until I found someone to take his place.

I had almost forgotten what it was like to write a check to the landlord every month. I had been living in the loft rent free. Felix Drinnan, who was the closest thing I had to an in-law—being all but married to my niece Alison—had magnanimously provided me with a place to live in the building he owned. One of three buildings that he owned, actually. The others, as far as I knew, were much more profitable invest-ments.

I had come to rely more and more on Felix and Alison. And not just for housing. They had been of invaluable help to me on a cou-ple of my cases. Besides that, I loved them both. And right now I missed them both.

Alison had a burgeoning career as a fash-ion model. She had jetted off to Japan to do a runway show, and Felix had accompanied her. I smiled, thinking of the truckload of antiques and sundry collectibles he was sure to bring back at the end of the trip.

I tore up the check and wrote another for a *much* smaller amount.

I had forgotten a lot of things, it appeared. Like what it was like to have a job. I'd been spending my pennies on things for the loft; little gifts for Alison and Felix; all those endless and endlessly tempting trifles that greet you everywhere you look in the Village— everything from imported ale to first editions to vintage clothing.

All that would have to stop now, wouldn't it? I'd have to start beating the bushes for work. I made a vow to speak to my agent before the end of the day, and to start calling all my cat-sitting clients, working my way methodically from "Abelson" to "Zwick."

Okay, Alison and Felix weren't the only old standbys I missed.

These last two days I had thought a lot about Tony. But I hadn't tried to reach him. And he had not called me. I wouldn't let myself think too much about questions like Would I ever see him again? Would we make up? What would life be like without him? Whose fault was it, anyway?

I made myself some lunch—tuna. The

cats begged me to share with them. I said no, sorry. I had only one can.

While I was drinking lemonade and indulging in a few of the homemade chocolate gingersnaps they sell at the high-tone deli next to the Hudson Street post office, the telephone rang again.

I picked it up immediately.

"Hallo, hallo! Is Al-eeece talking? Al-eeece Nestleton?" the heavily accented voice on the other end of the line asked.

"Yes, this is Alice Nestleton."

"We have a job for brilliant actress like yourself."

"What did you say? What job?"

"You tour People's Republic in avant-garde production of *Trojan Women*, yes? You like?"

"Are you serious?"

"Is you who must be serious, *bubbala*. One thing only: production is topless. Okay with you?"

"Who the hell is this?"

"Nora Karroll, you dope. Come to dinner."

I brought daffodils. Common daffodils. But dozens of them. They looked wonderful on the table near the kitchen where Nora and I were having our meal.

"So what happened with Harvey Keitel?" Nora asked me as one of the waiters set our drinks in front of us.

The waiter looked at me expectantly, eager to hear my answer.

"Nora, I think you'd better stop referring to Tony as Harvey Keitel. It just causes trouble."

She laughed mischievously. "Okay. But seriously, what happened? Have you heard from him?"

I shook my head.

"Don't want to talk about it, huh?"

I shook it again.

"We're having crab cakes, Alice . . . among other things," Nora said. "Hope you like 'em. I let the sous chef take over tonight. I got a recipe that's so easy to follow, it's foolproof. Well, up to a point. I guess you have to have a feel for food. You know what I mean?"

"Not really, Nora. I'm not much of a cook. I just like to eat the stuff."

Five minutes later, while I was doing just that—the crab cakes were quite wonderful— the gourmet detective walked in. It was Lieutenant Stoner from the precinct house down the block, the one who interviewed Basillio and me the night of John's murder.

He was heading straight for our table.

I was both surprised and not surprised to see him in Nora's place. On the one hand, he had recommended the food here. But on the other hand, I never actually expected to run into him.

Funny, when I saw him striding toward us, I naturally assumed he had tracked me down and was bringing some sort of news to me—probably bad.

But I was mistaken. He was joining us for dinner!

"Alice, this is my buddy Aaron Stoner. He's a cop. A cop with a hell of a palate, I might add."

I held out my hand, unsure whether to pretend I didn't know him.

But Stoner set things right. "Well, imagine this," he said, not exactly laughing but showing lots of strong, sharp teeth. "Actually, Nora, Alice and I have met before. *I've* had the pleasure," he said, and then added, "to some extent, that is."

Whereupon he broke into a real grin.

"You love to make the girls blush, don't you, you cajun rascal?" Nora teased him.

"He's no more cajun than you are, Alice," she told me over her shoulder. "I just like to call him that because he's a New Orleans boy . . . Oh, oh my goodness!" Nora suddenly exclaimed. "I just remembered something I hadn't thought of in a hundred years, Alice."

"What's that?"

"My turn as Baby Doll in the Williams' play. That *awful* frigging southern accent I turned on. Was I the absolute pits or what?"

"Don't be so hard on yourself," I said. "Accents are treacherous. In fact, I don't even believe in them."

"Yes, I remember that was one of your nutty theories."

"Is Alice a nut?" Stoner asked. "She looks to me like a lady with her feet on the ground."

"Well, thanks, Lieutenant Stoner."

"Of course," he continued addressing Nora, "she *is* an actress. She could be crazy as a goonybird."

I broke in on their laughter. "Nora, listen—and you, too, Lieutenant—one thing about me I never told you," I said very grimly. "I never took well to being teased. Ever since I was a child. I just never knew how to stand up under it."

Both Stoner and Nora shrank away in embarrassment.

We were halfway through our grilled lamb salad before I let them off the hook and told them I was just having a little fun with them.

"It's my ingenue *shtick*," I explained. "I don't use it too often."

Then I got serious.

"I know it might be something you don't want to talk about, Lieutenant Stoner," I said, "but what's the latest on the Adda Krispus story? Are you any closer to knowing why she shot John?"

"It's okay," he answered. "I can talk about it—what there is to talk about. Adda Krispus is still refusing legal counsel. She doesn't want a plea bargain and she doesn't want a trial and she doesn't want a priest. She freely admits to killing Mr. Cerise but refuses to say why. It's like they say in the papers, she shows no remorse.

" 'Course, her family's demanding private psychiatric testing and everything else in the garden. But the lady won't budge. She don't want no part of it.

"She could get ninety-nine years, but she doesn't seem to mind that a bit. I don't know—she did something pretty cuckoo, but the doctors say her mind is sound. She seems to be as sane as any of the rest of us.

"My guess is that she'll die in prison."

"My God, how absurd," I said. I didn't know how else to characterize his report.

"What about you?" Stoner asked me. "Have you come up with any reasons for Mr. Cerise lying about who he was?"

"No."

The answer might be a little more complicated than a flat "no." But I didn't know Stoner very well; it was too early in the relationship to go into the call I'd received from Glenda Fuchs—into the cat connection. The last thing I needed was for Stoner to truly believe I was a nut.

"You're having some, aren't you, Alice?"

Nora's question interrupted the continental drift my poor mind had taken.

"Some what, Nora?" I asked.

"Some *crème brûlée.*"

"Not this time, Nora. You know, I can no longer button those pants I had on the other day."

"Oh pish," she said. "Aaron, Alice used to be the skinniest old stringbean. I think she looks much better now, with a bit of meat on her bones."

The look in Lieutenant Stoner's eyes told me that he agreed with Nora. He opened his mouth, and my guess was that he was just about to say how much he agreed with her

. . . but his beeper went off at just that moment.

He excused himself and went to phone the station.

Nora was still trying to persuade me to have dessert when he got back.

"I guess I do have an update for you after all," Stoner said, looking directly at me.

"What's happened? Did she say why she did it?"

"No. Not her. It's the old man—Adda Krispus's husband—he died three hours ago."

Chapter 6

The brutal weather broke that first week of September.

It looked as though we were going to have a genuine autumn, which was becoming more and more rare in New York.

That nice cleanness was in the air.

But so was the faint heartache that beautiful spring or fall days can bring on.

The death of Peter Krispus seemed to put a kind of cap on the John Cerise tragedy. I had begun to deal with the loss, and the process of forgetting had already started.

No word from Tony.

That surprised me. We'd had fights before. We'd been out of touch before. But nothing like this had ever happened.

He was part of the faint heartache, too. But the healing process was setting in for that as well. Everything must change. All things must pass. I had had a long time with Basillio—a long time and often a good time. But it had come to an end.

I was sorry about it. I missed him. It still hurt. But the patient was expected to make a full recovery, thank you.

The last week in August, I did a voiceover for a new feminine hygiene product. To this day, I'm not sure what it purports to cure. Anyhow, they liked me at the studio, my agent said, and maybe there would be more work before the end of the year.

Two separate cat-sitting clients had to take unexpected trips. So I was bringing in a little money for taking care of Barbarella, a gray Persian who lived in Zeckendorf Towers, and Mitsuko, a lovely brown shorthair all the way down at Battery Park City.

I thanked my lucky stars for bringing Nora Karroll back into my life. She was such a good friend to me. She supplied everything from free lunches to free tickets.

Lately she'd been working on the book for a musical. It was loosely based on her early days in show business. She passed the pages from her first draft on to me practically as they came out of the typewriter. I knew nothing about the musical theater, really; didn't know whether her ideas were good or terrible. But it was fun to meet with her and discuss the project.

I stood for a while looking out the loft window. Yes, it did look like a lovely day.

I wasn't in the mood to do any serious end-of-season cleaning, but I did gather a bagful of sweaters and skirts and trousers for the dry cleaners. I left the morning dishes in the sink, turned on the answering machine, and waved good-bye to Bushy. The last time I saw Pancho, he was disappearing under the sink.

It felt good to be outdoors. Not a trace of mugginess. I decided to walk to Battery Park instead of hopping on the subway later, when it was time to feed Mitsuko.

When I passed the magazine store on Hudson Street, I took my usual gander at the array of glossy publications in the window. One of these days, I wagered, I'd see Alison's face on the cover of a slick fashion magazine.

The daily papers were stacked in bins on the sidewalk in front of the shop. I made a quick survey of the headlines of each of New York's big dailies.

The ones on the *Times* were too modest to bother with. The smallness of the type made it appear that nothing terribly important was happening.

It was one of the *Post* headlines that stopped me in my tracks:

WAY-OUT WRITER LEAVES MILLIONS TO CATS!

And in slightly smaller type beneath it:

OFF B'WAY BARD P.N. KRISPUS POSED AS PAUPER

I picked up the paper and looked into the craggy face of the man pictured. He was younger in the photograph, which must have been a good fifteen years old, but the face was undoubtedly that of Peter Nelson Krispus.

The story continued on page 3. I read every word.

• Krispus, who in his last years had come to be known as a charity case, and in whose behalf annual fund-raising parties were held, had in truth been a millionaire.

• He had left an estate of more than $2 million to his two whimsically named cats, George Bernard and Shaw.

• The will provided for a country house

for the felines, complete with their own cook, servant, and vet services.

• Named as executor of the will was a young Broadway dancer, Bobbi Ann Budd.

• Krispus's stunned and outraged survivors—including Merlin Krispus, elder son, and Hume Krispus, his brother—have announced plans to contest the will, claiming that Miss Budd had obviously exerted undue influence on their father.

• Having accused the young dancer of enticing a deranged old man with sex, and describing her as a "gold digger," the Krispus sons admit that they have never met the young woman.

• In a bizarre, related story, the old man's widow, Adda Krispus, is currently under arrest without bail, pending trial on murder charges. Apparently, she has already admitted killing a Manhattan man who was a guest in the Krispus home earlier this summer. Authorities say they have so far not ascertained the motive for the killing and the accused continues to refuse counsel or to speak to anyone about the crime.

I stood there in the middle of the pavement, the wind blowing across my shoulders, reading a newspaper I hadn't paid for, probably with my jaw gaping open.

I paid for the *Post.* And the *Times* and the *Daily News* and *Newsday* as well.

Then I beat it back home.

I didn't even stop for chocolate gingersnaps.

Some of the newspapers made more of the event than others. I read every account of the story.

It was one of those times when the most natural thing in the world would be to pick up the telephone and call someone to talk about what you'd just learned. But I couldn't. I couldn't think of a thing to say.

Apparently, Adda Krispus was not the only crazy person in that family.

I piled the newspapers near the trash can.

I felt terrible. And numb. And utterly baffled.

I took off my shoes and stretched out on the bed, at a loss.

Both cats appeared a minute later. They were making a rare appearance as a duo. Maybe Bushy had been giving Pancho a few sensitivity pointers. The two of them sniffed around at my toes for a while and then settled in for naps.

I envied them. It would be nice to sleep now, escape, forget.

Why did I feel the need to escape? Because I felt so alone, I guess. What was the matter with me? This kind of mopey behavior wasn't me at all. What kind of idiot was I turning into? What was stopping me from opening a book, going for a walk, doing any of the dozens of things that usually filled my life?

In a few minutes I got up and began my pacing ritual. When I got bored with that, I rushed over to the trash and retrieved all the newspapers.

A second reading of the coverage of Peter Nelson Krispus's bizarre deception and the details of his strange bequest didn't really clear anything up. All it did was pull me in further—baffle me more.

But it did make me aware—for the first time—of the obvious connection between Krispus and John Cerise: cats.

Cats! Krispus had left his mysterious fortune to his cats. John Cerise had been dedicated to cats. They were his life.

This time my pacing was more purposeful. Not only was I trying to fit John into the puzzle of the mysterious Krispus fortune and the will—I was once again focused on John's incomprehensible denial of who he was. How did that fit?

It was hard to think, because once again

the image of Adda Krispus raising the gun had begun to intrude. That had a way of pushing everything calm and logical out of my head.

I grabbed a pencil and notepad and began to list every single thing that had occurred since the day of the murder. I hadn't got very far when the phone rang.

The caller was breathless, overanxious. But it wasn't another sales call.

It was Glenda Fuchs, from OAC, the cat rescue organization.

"I need your help, Miss Nestleton," she said, a note of desperation in her voice.

What was I supposed to do—apologize for the paltry donation I had made?

Before I could think of the words, though, she interrupted me.

"I know it's an imposition, but I was hoping you could help me out with a favor. I need to see you."

I didn't answer for a minute. Maybe she *did* expect me to beg with a tin can. Then I said, "All right."

"Good. Can you come to see me this afternoon?"

"I suppose so. Where do you live?"

"On Amsterdam. But that doesn't matter now. I'm not at home."

"Where are you?"

"The hospital. Lenox Hill. Do you know where it is?"

"Yes, but . . . are you all right? What happened?"

"Nothing very good. I'll be expecting you."

Chapter 7

There was no time to play with Mitsuko in her bamboo dollhouse. I made a furious survey of her owner's apartment, fed the cat, locked up, and left the apartment.

I'd make it up to lonely Mitsuko some other day.

Nora was waiting for me on the sidewalk when my cab pulled up at her doorman building on West 57th Street. She had agreed to accompany me to the hospital.

"Agreed" is the wrong word. When I phoned her to report on all the bizarre developments of the day, she insisted on coming with me to the hospital. Not only was she eager to help, she seemed to look at the whole thing as one of my "nutty" adventures, which she couldn't wait to share.

"I suppose I don't have to tell you that you

have an admirer," she confided as we sat in the back of the taxi.

"You'll have to be a little more specific, Nora," I said.

"Aaron," she answered impatiently. "Who do you think I'm talking about—Cole Porter?"

"Lieutenant Stoner, you mean."

I guess I was being just a tad coy. I knew who she meant all along.

"Yes," said she. "Aaron Stoner. You're all he talks about."

"Really?"

"Well, not *absolutely* all. But practically. He says he heard from another cop who heard from somebody else that you're an investigator. Wonders why you never told him yourself. Anyway, you didn't even tell me you had worked as a consultant to the police. You have been busy all these years, haven't you?"

"I suppose so. But, to be honest, my consultancy wasn't exactly a love fest between me and the NYPD. I broke the case in the end, but it got pretty unpleasant. They gave me a name I didn't appreciate."

"What name?"

"Cat Woman."

Nora hooted.

I laughed a little myself. "It's funny, the things you find yourself doing when you're an out-of-work actor."

"Beats waitressing, doesn't it?"

"Believe me, Nora, you've never had a waitress as bad as the waitress I would make."

"What about the present caper?" she asked.

"Which one?" I said.

"I mean Glenda, the Good Witch. You know, the Case of the Lenox Hill Cat Goddess."

"This *isn't* a caper, Nora. I'm just trying to help someone who's doing admirable work, rescuing cats."

"Oh," she said, disappointment in her voice. "I was hoping I could help you solve a mystery. I always wanted to play Effie, Sam Spade's secretary . . . or Della Street."

"You're incorrigible, Nora. Not only won't you be Della Street. You won't even be Della Reese."

I had never met Glenda Fuchs. So of course I had no point of comparison. But I could pretty safely say she wasn't looking her best that day.

She looked, in a word, horrible. She was a

mass of bruises and one arm was in a for-
midable, stiff white cast.

Apparently, she had been sideswiped by a
Toyota as she stood waiting for a cab early
that morning. It was an ugly hit-and-run.

"I'm sorry we're meeting this way, Miss
Nestleton," she said groggily.

"Don't worry about it," I told her.

"Yes," Nora said, "you're forgiven for not
shaking hands."

Glenda Fuchs tried to laugh, but I think
the effort must have hurt. Her bottom lip
was split.

"I've told you a little bit about OAC, haven't
I, Miss Nestleton?" the injured woman said.

"Yes. And please call me Alice."

"Well, at the moment we're centering our
efforts on Fort Tryon Park, where there's a
huge feline population. We want to trap and
neuter the ferals because the city is threatening to kill them. We've got to raise more
money.

"This *would* have to happen just when the
organization is so shorthanded! It's the end
of the summer. Everybody's out of town. Or
just arriving back in town. Or busy with
other charity work. Or whatever. I've had a
million things to do. All the last-minute
work was resting squarely on my shoul-

ders . . . and now . . . this. It makes me so mad!"

"It's too bad your organization doesn't have an angel," Nora put in. "Why couldn't that nut Peter Nelson Krispus have left your wild cats a few hundred thousand—as long as he had such a soft spot for his own cats."

Glenda's face reddened suddenly. "Oh, please!" she said angrily. "Don't even mention that idiot's name to me right now. With all the worthy causes in the world—not to mention OAC—he had to go and leave a fortune to carry out some screwy bequest like that. Animals don't need a castle to live in. They just need a clean, safe home and someone to care for them. His cats already had that—even if it was just a normal old tenement apartment in Hell's Kitchen."

"I know, I know," I said, trying to soothe her. "But you'd better take it easy for now. Why don't you tell us how we can help, and then you can get some rest."

"Yes, you're right," Glenda agreed. "I was on the way to the OAC office when I was hit. I'd like you to go over there and do a couple of things. Get me my bag from the closet over there and I'll give you the keys."

Nora went to the closet and fetched the bag.

"First," Glenda said, taking a deep breath, "there's a box of envelopes—they're already stuffed. They're our fund-raising letters. They need to be sealed and taken to the post office for bulk mailing.

"And then, if you could, take the copy for our new brochure to the printer on Broadway. You'll find the address on the board right next to the telephone. The printer gives us a break on prices, but he's got to have the job in the next day or two, before he gets too busy with other things.

"Is that too much?"

"Of course not," I said. "We'll do it right now. Before the post office closes."

We left Glenda with a few back issues of *People* magazine, which Nora had found in the nurses' lounge down the hall. She managed to look both anxious and drowsy. I was hoping she'd drift off to sleep soon.

As she waved good-bye and thanked us again, I couldn't help thinking that she did look a bit like Glenda, the good witch in *The Wizard of Oz.*

The OAC office was a far cry from Rockefeller Foundation. I understood that OAC was a poor little organization hungry for funds, but I hadn't expected anything quite so . . . pitiful.

Nora and I used the keys Glenda had given us and opened the door of the sparsely furnished cubicle in a run-down office building far west on 56th Street. It was not far from Nora's own home, but it was of a different world.

I had no trouble locating the box of fund-raising appeals. We made quick work of sealing the envelopes and rubber-banding them for the post office.

I took the card with the printer's name and address down from the bulletin board and copied the information into my notebook. Then I found the pasteup for the brochure.

It wasn't until we were almost ready to turn out the lights and leave that I looked closely at the stray sheet of letterhead stationery that was lying on the desk. In small letters at the top of the page were listed all the names of the OAC board of directors.

Glenda Fuchs's name was there, of course. So was John Cerise's. And, among the other six, a name that startled the hell out of me: Merlin Krispus.

Now, how many men in New York had the

name Merlin Krispus? I didn't need to consult the white pages to answer that one.

Peter Nelson Krispus's older son, Merlin, was serving on the board of directors of OAC. He had been a colleague of John Cerise. Even if the board members never really sat face to face, how likely was it that Merlin had never even heard of John Cerise?

I thought back to my meeting with the members of the Krispus family . . . in that death house . . . the house of liars.

After we'd carried out all Glenda's instructions, Nora and I repaired to the bistro.

While she was talking over the evening menu with her assistant, I made a call to Glenda Fuchs. I wanted to inquire about her health and assure her that we'd taken care of everything. But I also wanted to ask some questions about Merlin Krispus.

Yes, Glenda told me, of course she knew Merlin. He'd been on the board for a few years now. In fact, it was John Cerise who had recommended him.

So Merlin had lied. There was the proof. But why?

I hung up and let Glenda get back to her liquid dinner.

I was puzzled. Why did Merlin lie? What would have been the harm in admitting he knew John? No one was accusing him of anything. After all, there was no question that he had played any part in John's death. We all knew Adda Krispus was responsible for that.

I looked over and saw Nora waiting for me at the bar.

What about the present caper? she had joked earlier. Was this going to turn into a caper, a real investigation?

I didn't think in those corny old private-eye terms. Yet I could sense that something was terribly wrong. I knew that Merlin—and the other family members—were lying for some very real reasons they didn't want me to know about. And I owed it to John to find out what those reasons were.

For him, and for me, I needed to find out what was going on.

I looked over at Nora again.

Maybe she was going to get to be Della Street, after all.

Chapter 8

It was hard to tell whether the shop was open or closed.

I thought I saw a dim light inside, but I couldn't be sure.

The doorknob did not turn when I tried it. I didn't see a bell. I didn't see a sign listing the store's hours. One didn't knock on shop doors, the way one knocked on bedroom doors . . . did one?

Merlin Krispus was the proprietor of an antiques store just off 9th Avenue, on 27th Street. It was midday, and the middle of the week. You'd think a shop like his would be open now, if ever.

I knocked.

"It's open!"

At least, that's what I thought I heard. The voice was muffled and sounded a mile away.

I tried the door again. This time it opened.

Merlin Krispus stood with his back to me. He was polishing a rolltop desk with an oily cloth.

"Hello, Mr. Krispus," I said firmly.

Only then did he turn toward me.

"I'm Alice Nestleton. We met at—"

"Yes, I know. How are you, Miss Nestleton?"

"I'm all right. I've been better, but on the whole I'm all right."

"So good of you to visit, Miss Nestleton. Are you in the market for a beautiful padded chaise longue? I got one in only yesterday."

"Thank you, but I'm not here to shop."

"Ah."

He looked blankly at me, just as his sister-in-law Jane had done the last time I'd visited the Krispus apartment.

"I can see you're very busy, Mr. Krispus. So I'll come to the point right away."

I paused, in spite of what I had just said.

There was no sign that he had caught my attempt at irony, and no sign of impatience in his manner, either. He merely waited for me to go on.

"The point is," I continued, "that you and the rest of your family denied knowing John Cerise, the man your mother shot. I can't speak for the rest of your family, Mr. Krispus, but it appears that you know—knew—John very well. Well enough, anyway, for him to recruit you as a member of the Our Alley Cats organization. You serve on its board of directors, and so did John."

Merlin never batted an eye. He didn't deny. He didn't affirm. He didn't even ask how I found him. (Simple enough—the phone book listed both his home and business addresses.) He didn't speak. He didn't move.

"I'm here to find out why you lied, Merlin. What was the point?"

There was the slightest movement of his body then. He half turned and picked up his cigarette pack from a nearby table.

At last he spoke, after he had located a book of matches in his pants pocket. "If I remember correctly, you said you were an actress."

"That's right. So what?"

A rather hideous expression began to move across his face then. It was one of full, unmitigated contempt.

"I should have known the minute you walked into my parents' home," Merlin spat out. "Even before Luther identified your profession with one of his cheap seduction techniques. You and your kind make me sick. I've had to put up with you preposterous *theater* people all my life! Father subjected us to the worst kind of poverty and humiliation, while he treated the lot of you hustlers like gods or something."

"What on earth are you talking about?" I said in disbelief.

"I'll tell you what I'm talking about! Only an actor would be so self-important . . . so presumptuous . . . so rude. No one else would think himself entitled to walk into my dying father's house and dare to question us the way you did. My mother in great trouble and my father deathly ill, and you come barging into our lives and—"

I was unprepared. Unprepared for Merlin's reaction, and unprepared for the response it evoked in me.

Suddenly I was shouting wildly at him:

"There's really no point in behaving this way to me, Merlin. This is inexcusable! I did nothing to you and your family . . . not half of what I should have done, anyway. Your little tirade is nothing but your guilty conscience speaking! You're hiding something about John's death and you know it. And furthermore, mister, I'm not the one who caused your mother's troubles. So don't take it out on me!"

Even in the heat of my screaming fit, I could hear something—a scraping noise—behind the curtain at the back of the shop.

For a second, fear overtook me. I half expected Adda Krispus to appear and shout "Look!"

I half expected to be shot right where I stood.

Merlin knew I heard it. I could tell by the way he switched gears.

"We're both upset, Miss Nestleton," he said, playing the cool-headed mediator. In fact, we're both totally overexcited. I'm not at my best when I'm emotional like this. Why don't we try holding this conversation at another time?"

No one stepped out of the shadows. All was quiet back there.

"I don't think so," I answered Merlin's invitation. "I don't think I like the way you make conversation, Merlin."

"Suit yourself," he mumbled.

"Why don't I talk to whoever is behind that curtain instead?" I suggested.

"That curtain and what is behind it are none of your business." He was growing angry all over again. "It's just as I said, isn't

it? You people are the most arrogant
. . . presumptuous—"

"Knock it off, Merlin," I cut him off. Then I
called toward the back: "Come out and face
me, why don't you? Or are you all cowards
and liars?"

"Harsh words, Miss Nestleton," said Hume
Krispus as he stepped into the room.

His wife Jane was a step behind him. She
remained silent.

"Harsh words seem to be called for," I
replied. "Well, isn't there one of you who'll
admit you knew John Cerise? Or, more important, why he was murdered?"

"Please go," Merlin said simply. "We've
nothing further to say to you."

"It won't be so easy the next time," I said,
trying to sound threatening, tough.

"Don't make us call the police, Miss
Nestleton," Hume said.

I laughed at him. "Oh, I don't think you
want to do that, do you?"

"Please go," Merlin repeated slowly, "and
leave our family alone."

What choice did I have?

I turned and walked out.

I blew it, as Tony Basillio might have said.

And he'd be right. I blew it. I lost my cool.
My threats had not worked.

I walked up the block and stood there for a few moments, trying to decide what my next move should be.

Families. Families were tricky. They might fight amongst themselves like cats and dogs. Brother against brother. Mother against daughter. All the possible combinations. But then they might suddenly decide to be loyal, to stick together at all costs—even if it's in the service of some terrible goal. Fathers stopped bullets meant for their outlaw sons. Some wives happily lied to give their husbands a much-needed alibi. Others wanted to personally stuff their spouses' neck in the noose. It was all so hard to predict.

These Krispus people were a real problem.

There was someone in the Krispus apartment that day who wasn't a family member, however: the oily would-be seducer they called Luther.

Luther Kaminecki had looked at my palm and, as if by magic, declared that I was an actress.

Luckily, I didn't believe in magic.

Maybe Kaminecki would present the same problem. If he was presumptuous enough, to use Merlin's word, to think of himself as a Krispus family member, he would probably stonewall me, too.

On the other hand, the way they had treated him was not particularly loving or familial. Maybe he resented that. If he resented it enough, I just might be able to get him to talk to me about the Krispuses and John Cerise— assuming he knew more than he let on.

I might. Certainly it was worth a try. If I could find him.

The ream of newsprint I'd read the other day, when the news of Peter Nelson Krispus's will first broke, began to unroll inside my head.

A couple of articles had mentioned in passing that Luther Kaminecki was working on a biography of P.N. Krispus. I seemed to recall that the *Post* coverage referred to Kaminecki as a part-time teacher. I was trying to remember where he taught.

Merlin's shop was in the heart of Chelsea. I knew that there was a public library no more than a ten-minute walk away. They'd have the issue I was looking for.

I'd been on the so-called campus of Hunter College a couple of times before. Since the school was located in the center of one of the busiest districts in the city, Lexington Avenue in the mid-60s, it was something of a stretch to call it a campus at all.

It took a while to decipher the class schedule the young woman in the information office handed me, but I was finally able to determine that Luther Kaminecki was on campus twice a week. He taught an Introduction to Drama course on one day and a Gilbert and Sullivan class on the other. Today was G&S.

His office was on the fourth floor. By the time I reached it, the hour for the class to begin was just striking.

I saw him hurriedly locking the office door behind him, rushing for the staircase. I called his name loudly.

Luther's eyes widened when he caught sight of me. He broke into a sly grin.

"What a treat!" he said before I could utter a word. "It's the beautiful actress from . . . from . . . uh . . ."

"Minnesota," I said.

"What?"

"Never mind, Mr. Kaminecki. I realize you're in a hurry, but I wonder if I might have a minute of your time.

I'm afraid not, my dear Miss . . ."

"Alice Nestleton," I supplied.

Mr. Kaminecki seemed to love pretending he was bad with names.

"Oh yes. What a lovely name," he said patronizingly. "But I am late for class, madam. My students are waiting."

"Yes, I understand, Mr. Kaminecki. And if you could just answer a couple of questions about the Krispus family, I'll let you go on your way."

His eyes misted over. "Krispus. Oh yes, Krispus. What a loss, what a loss," he said, shaking his head.

"Um. Indeed. But I was thinking more about Merlin Krispus than the late Peter Nelson."

"Merlin? What about Merlin?"

"I've discovered that he knew John Cerise, the man Adda Krispus shot to death. You remember that, don't you, Mr. Kaminecki? And you remember my mentioning John's name to you?"

He waited awhile before answering, "Perhaps."

"Well, Merlin insists that he did not know John Cerise. Can you explain that? Even a guess?"

I had gradually maneuvered my body so that I was blocking his path to the stairwell.

Kaminecki turned his chipped-tooth smile on again. "My dear, I think perhaps I do recall Mr. Cerise. Where could my mind have been before? Mr. Cerise—which, interestingly enough, means cherry in French—was Peter's favorite masseur, wasn't he? The chap who used to arrive like an angel in white sweatpants and alleviate so much of the master's pain. He was a strapping young fellow, wasn't he—about twenty-five years old? Blond?"

"What a memory you have, Mr. Kaminecki," I said falsely. "Does this fantasy mean that Merlin has already phoned to warn you not to talk to me?"

He pulled a pair of spectacles from his vest pocket at that moment and placed them on his face, looking very much like the absentminded professor.

Suddenly the absentmindedness vanished and he looked me up and down in that chop-licking way. He said dismissively: "As for myself, I prefer ugly actresses." He adjusted his eyeglasses then.

"Must run now, lovely Miss Nettleton. I'm very late."

"Not *Nettleton*, dear Mr. Kaminecki," I corrected him, being a bit patronizing myself. "That's a different lovely actress."

He bustled off like the March hare.

*   *   *

Lydia Adamson

Pancho and Bushy were a little miffed at me. They expect me home at a certain hour and when I don't appear as planned, they get huffy.

I pulled out all the stops with the 79-cents-a-can food. That placated them some.

I drank an entire quart of apple juice straight from the bottle.

I was tired. Tired and frustrated.

I had just taken off my shoes and stretched out on the bed when the phone rang.

I let the machine answer. I heard Nora's voice after the beep.

Halfway through her message—she was chastising me severely for not keeping her posted on the "caper"—I picked up.

She listened quietly while I went over the events of the day—going to Merlin's shop; the surprise appearance of Hume and Jane Krispus; tracking Kaminecki down at the college; the stupid act he put on.

"Well," she said with a sigh at the end of my story, "all I can say is 'tsk, tsk, tsk, Alice.' "

"What do you mean?"

"I mean, you've certainly been less than the ideal little peeper today, haven't you? You haven't bribed, intimidated, beat up, or slept with a single suspect."

"Oh, that. Well, if you remember, Nora, you're the one with the Sam Spade fixation. Not me."

"That may be true, honey. But at least Sam always keeps his eye on the ball."

I think I've just been insulted, thought I.

"Just what are you getting at, Nora?"

"All I'm saying is, you're going off in the wrong direction. You're wasting your time."

"I beg your pardon! Who's the investigator here, Nora—me or you?"

"Take it easy, Alice. What I mean is that the Krispus nuts are a waste of time *at the moment*. They're going to tell you nothing. Forget their secrets for a moment and concentrate on your friend John's secrets."

I hung on, saying nothing, weighing her words.

"As a matter of fact," Nora added, "maybe he wasn't your friend at all."

"But he was, Nora. John was my friend."

"Sure he was. But maybe your friend wasn't John. Maybe you had no idea who that man really was."

So I hadn't known John Cerise at all. That was an upsetting thought. Unfortunately, though, I understood exactly what Nora meant.

It stung a little, but she was outthinking me—outsleuthing me.

After my conversation with Nora, I checked with Glenda Fuchs again. She was on the mend. And there was nothing wrong with her memory; she still maintained that John had lived in a sublet apartment on West End Avenue. She couldn't remember the address exactly, but she was sure the building was at 92nd Street.

I thanked her, told her to take care of herself, and hung up.

I was tired and wanted to sleep, but I couldn't turn off my thoughts. Indeed, the more I thought about Nora's theory, the more sense it made.

And the more nervous and torn I became.

Digging into John's life wasn't what I had intended at all. It was disrespectful. And dangerous.

What if I found out all kinds of awful things about him? That he was a check forger . . . a bigamist . . . a killer.

It would destroy my memories of him. It would mean that nothing had been real. That I had been taken in.

But I had to stop thinking that way—thinking of myself. The case wasn't about me. It was about learning the answer to John's murder. It was about seeking justice for John—whoever he was.

Chapter 9

I met Nora in Riverside Park the next morning.

Each day of the early autumn was clearer and more beautiful than the last.

We sat on a bench drinking coffee from paper containers and watching the children play. We were deciding on a strategy for gaining entry to the apartment where John Cerise had lived until Adda Krispus ended his life.

"No problem," Nora said breezily. "Fifty bucks."

"Fifty bucks for what?" I asked.

"For the doorman, of course."

"Oh, yes. Right."

"We knew that there were huge apartment buildings on two of the four corners of 92nd and West End. On the third corner a more moderate-size building. And on the last, a four-story brownstone that was empty and under renovations.

We figured that we'd never have the good luck of having the small building be the one John lived in. That was too much to hope for. It had to be one of the monsters.

Nora was dressed to the nines—fur jacket, heels, freshly painted red nails, and all. She had suggested when we spoke early that morning that I doll myself up as well. I had an inkling as to why she had made the request of me, so I complied. Our minds were now running along the same path so consistently that it was a little discombobulating.

I had forgotten how good an actress Nora could be. Hell, I'd nearly forgotten how good I was. We put on a nice performance. It was a question of appearing half haughty and half dizzy.

We told the doorman at the first building that we were the friends and Westchester neighbors of the original tenant of the apartment that a Mr. John Cerise had been subletting. We were aware that Mr. Cerise had passed away recently. As a favor to the original tenant, who was away in Europe at the moment, we had come to survey the place, with an eye to renting it out again. The trouble was, we had left the exact address back home in Westchester. All we knew was that the building was on one of these four corners.

The uniformed, elderly doorman was at a loss. He had no idea what we were talking about.

Bob Heath, the super at the huge building across the street, who looked more like a corporate executive than a building superintendent, recognized the name Cerise immediately.

"No, no, ladies," he corrected. "You don't mean the original *tenant*. You mean the original owner."

"Of course I mean the owner," Nora snapped at him. "That's exactly what I said—*owner*."

"Of course you did, Loretta," I said, casting an outraged glance at the super.

I pulled the keys to my own apartment out of my bag then and shook them in his face.

"If you'll just show us where it is . . ." I said to Mr. Heath. The whole thing smacked of buffoonery or slapstick. But it worked.

We took the elevator up to the eighth floor.

"Thank you," I said offhandedly when he deposited us at Apartment 8–E. And then I proceeded to fumble with the lock.

"Oh, for god's sake, Helen!" Nora barked

at me. "Don't tell me you brought the wrong ones. Here, let me look at those . . . Damnit, just as I thought! Those are the keys to the pool house. What are we going to do now? Oh, wait, wait, Mr. Heath!"

Bob Heath gave us a healthy helping of reverse *noblesse oblige*. He made us feel every bit the ninnies we were pretending to be. But eventually he opened the door for us.

To thank him for his help, Nora reached casually into her purse, fumbled for a few seconds, and came out with a crisp fifty-dollar bill, which she pressed into his hand. He looked down at it for a few seconds, with great affection.

Mr. Heath told us to let him know when we were ready to leave so that he could lock up behind us.

And there was something else, he said.

We turned toward him in unison.

He had assumed that the place would be nearly empty now, since Mr. Cerise's brother had showed up last week to go through his belongings. But, as we could see, the apartment was still full of John's things.

He couldn't explain why John's brother had "left all his stuff," but he hoped we weren't expecting him to haul it all away.

"No," I assured him. "We'll take care of that, Mr. Heath."

Nora and I exchanged glances as Mr. Heath closed the door behind him.

So a phantom brother had appeared last week. I didn't buy it.

It wasn't very likely that John had a brother who would have shown up out of nowhere. Where was this brother now? Why hadn't he contacted any of John's friends? Why hadn't he made any funeral arrangements?

We went over the apartment minutely, but we could find nothing out of the ordinary. Oh sure, in every apartment there is a confounding object—a piece of tasteless art, a quirky bit of furniture, a can of low-salt olives—that is uniquely the property of the tenant. There were odds and ends like that in John's place. But we were finding nothing more intriguing than a cheap Mexican vase on the bathroom windowsill.

I went over and flipped through the records and audiotapes on the rug near the stereo. There was the expected complement of classical and popular music, what you might find in any grown-up's home—Beethoven's Ninth . . . Ella Fitzgerald.

Then I found what appeared to be a tape for

children. The spine of the cassette case was hand lettered, not a commercially made tape.

Dumbo, the label read.

"Dumbo was an elephant, wasn't he? A cartoon elephant?"

Not a cartoon, Nora corrected me. Animation. "It was a Disney thing, back in the fifties."

It must have been the music—the soundtrack—from the film. Now, *that* was a little quirky.

Didn't sound much like John's taste.

I wondered if *Dumbo* had been John's favorite story as a child. But no, he wasn't a child in the fifties.

I had the sudden urge to listen to the tape, actually, but when I opened the case, it was empty.

When I spotted a second hand-lettered label, I looked closely at that case, too.

Pinocchio.

Also empty.

So was *Snow White.*

And so was *Lady and the Tramp.*

Maybe John had a brother, after all, and lots of nieces and nephews as well.

I got the last-minute inspiration to look inside the cassette player portion of the stereo setup; perhaps one of the tapes was in there.

No luck.

We went on searching.

We found an old postcard from a woman friend who was sending her love to John while honeymooning in the Bahamas.

We found a grocery list or two.

We found lots of indecipherable notes on OAC note paper.

And we found a paid receipt for $30, from a dance studio on Broadway. It covered a full week of dance classes!

Another unexpected quirk. I couldn't picture John Cerise dancing.

"Where is the studio, Nora? Do you know?"

She looked at the address. "Yeah, I think so. It's one of those places on the strip."

"What sort of strip?"

"Oh there's a gang of loft studios on Broadway, near all the theaters. You know, rehearsal spaces, ballet schools, tap classes, yoga, aerobics. You don't notice them unless you look up. They're mostly above stores or restaurants."

"What do you think about taking our ladies from Westchester act on the road?" I said.

"Have manicure, will travel," she replied.

"Let's be adventurous Westchester ladies and take the subway," I suggested.

The ride was less than six minutes long. We got out at the 50th Street IRT station and found the Legs Dance Studio two blocks up Broadway, at 52nd Street.

Everywhere we looked, someone in a leotard was stretching, squatting, pirouetting, or drinking Evian.

"I feel so ashamed, Alice," Nora said under her breath. "I'm hideously out of shape."

"Don't worry," I told her. "Nobody's looking at us. They think we're here to pick up our daughters . . . or our daughters' daughters."

"That really makes me feel better," quipped Nora.

"May I help you?" a lithe middle-aged woman in a sweatband and turquoise leotard asked.

I was holding the $30 receipt we'd found at my side.

"I think you can," I told the woman. "My name is Alice Nestleton. This is my friend Nora Karroll."

"Oh, yes," she said, peering at Nora. "You *are* Nora Karroll! You were in that Charles Strouse thing, weren't you? Back in 1965

. . . oh, let's see . . . maybe even before that . . . 1963, was it?"

"Sixty-five's far enough," Nora said, smiling.

"You were awfully good. It's a pleasure to meet you. Are you still performing?"

"Lord, no," Nora said, a bit sadly.

"Too bad. I'm Mia Hanson, by the way. I teach jazz dance and yoga."

"Nice to meet you," I said.

"You two decided to take a few brush-up classes? Get back in shape?" Mia asked.

"No, not that," I said. "Actually, we wanted to ask if you knew a friend of mine who died recently: John Cerise."

The name seemed to startle her.

"Yes," Mia said. "Of course I knew John. I knew him for years—well, I can't say he was an intimate friend, but he'd been coming to the studio for the last twenty years or so. He was a dear man. I adored him."

"So you can verify that this receipt is from your studio?" I handed the paper over to her.

"Sure it is. He paid either by the month or the week. John was a classic hoofer, from the old school. He hadn't been in a Broadway chorus line for over two decades, but he never let himself go."

I was stunned. Absolutely, flat-out stunned.

"Did you say Broadway?" I asked in a whisper.

"Yes," Mia answered.

"Did you say Broadway chorus line?"

"Yes," she repeated, confused. "Didn't you know he was a dancer?"

I merely shook my head.

"John was a pro," Mia said admiringly. "Like I said, he was taking lessons, keeping himself tuned, right up to—"

She stopped for a moment, her eyes moist, until the lump in her throat went away.

"I didn't even know he was . . . dead. . . for weeks after it happened. I wondered what had happened to him. One of the kids told me. She heard it over at Cozy. I don't read the papers much, you know."

I nodded and took back the receipt.

"What was the place you just mentioned— Cozy's?" I asked.

"A bar. A lot of kids hang out there. I don't drink anymore. Haven't been there in ages."

"Can you tell me where—"

Nora interrupted me. "It's okay," she said. "I know where it is."

Chapter 10

As we walked through the doors of the dark and cavernous saloon on 9th Avenue, Evita Perón—on tape, of course—was counseling Argentina in song, saying not to cry for her.

Apparently, the management at Cozy's bar was very fond of show tunes.

Nora reconfirmed what Mia had said. Many of the young Broadway singers and dancers—and a lot of show-biz hangers-on—drank at Cozy. Some weekends there were showcases held in the back room. Young cabaret performers often broke in their new acts here, to a friendly and supportive audience of their peers and pals.

"I don't get over here much," Nora told me, "but I know the bartender, Gus Michaels. He helped me out at the bistro a couple of times when I was shorthanded. Nice guy. I wonder if he'll recognize me in my wealthy matron drag."

I was only half listening to Nora. Something was nagging at me, some vague memory. "There's something oddly familiar about this place," I said as we walked the length of the dark wood bar. "I know I've never been here before, but there's just . . . something."

"It used to be a terrible joint, I think," Nora said, "back in the old old days. Nightly stabbings and so on. Hardly the kind of place a well-brought-up Westchester lass like you would have frequented."

"Of course!" I said. "That's what I'm remembering. This bar had a very bad reputation when we were all studying at the Workshop. I think Tony might have been here once or twice—trying to prove he was as macho as any Times Square denizen."

"Oh, really? And what happened?"

"I don't recall. But I'll bet if he witnessed a knife fight, he didn't come back again."

We both laughed.

"Actors!" Nora said with both annoyance and affection. "They're as bad as ballet dancers when it comes to proving they're not . . . you know . . . gay."

"That was one thing I never doubted about Tony. Quite the opposite, in fact. He must have been blessed—or cursed—with a few extra hormones. He can be a bit compulsive about . . . love. Which can be every bit as troublesome as a fella whose cup of tea you're not."

"Good title for a song, Alice . . . 'Something's the Matter with My Fella, His Cup of Tea I'm Not.' Let me write that down." She found her ballpoint pen and proceeded to do just that.

"Anyway, Alice, speaking of men," Nora said elliptically.

"Don't start in about Lieutenant Stoner again, Nora. I still haven't returned his call."

"Calls, don't you mean?" she teased.

"All right. Calls. He's left two messages inviting me to dinner. But I just can't think about that right now."

"And what about Tony? Is that the call you really want to return? Still?"

I shrugged. There was nothing to say about Tony. It was either too late or too soon to think about him. I didn't know which.

It was rather early in the afternoon, but there were quite a few customers about . . . eating hamburgers mostly, and drinking Bloody Marys or steins of beer. For a lot of performers, especially if they were working, this was breakfast time.

I looked around the refurbished room. I

couldn't see a jukebox. But there was a lovely melody on the tape now.

"What's that song, Nora? It's nice."

"It's from *Pacific Overtures*. You know, Sondheim. I love him."

"He's sort of an intellectual songwriter, isn't that what they say? You know how ignorant I am about music."

"Intellectual? I don't know about that—I guess you might call him that. He's different, that's for sure. Sophisticated. Nobody else writes songs like that. Although a lot of them try. Hell, all I know is, I like him. If I were fifteen years younger, maybe I'd be a leading light in one of his shows."

"You're not a dinosaur, Nora. Why couldn't you be in one of his shows now?"

She laughed. "Well, I suppose I could be one of the old broads in *Follies*. Or I could play Desiree."

"Who's that?"

"The aging actress—the mistress—in Night Music. Glynis Johns played her on Broadway. You know . . . *A Little Night Music*."

I shook my head. "Sorry. I told you you were talking to an ignoramus."

"Well, not about everything," she said generously. "You're no ignoramus about investigative work. And as soon as we get our booze, I've got questions for you."

"But can I answer them?" I said. "They're all about John Cerise, right? And what happened today? As a matter of fact, I probably have the same questions myself."

"So what's your considered opinion, then?" Nora said. "What was the big deal with having been a hoofer on Broadway? Why do you think John wouldn't have told you that?"

"Good question, Nora. Especially since he knew very well I was in the business myself. It would be even more reason for him to tell me."

"Hey, Nora!"

A muscular man with light hair, fortyish, was suddenly at our table.

"Gus!" Nora greeted him warmly. "How are you? This is my buddy Alice."

We shook hands.

"You look great, Nora. How's business?" he asked.

"Not bad. I'll tell you all the gossip in a minute. But first, who do you have to know to get a drink around here?"

"Oh, sorry, love. I'll take care of it myself. What are you drinking?"

"Keep it simple. Two ales—all right with

you, Alice? And let us see a couple of menus."

Gus hurried away.

"I think I can anticipate your next question," I told Nora. "Namely, was John a criminal of some kind? Was he hiding his past as a dancer because there was something shady attached to it?"

"So far, so good," she said. "That was question number two."

"Next," I continued, "And this is a big one, a key one: Did John have something to do with Peter Krispus's secret fortune?"

"Absolutely right."

"And last, was the mysterious brother who went over John's things in the apartment really one of the Krispus brothers—or maybe even that weird Luther Kaminecki."

"Bingo! Give that little girl her dollie. Those are exactly my questions."

And mine, I thought.

Gus returned with our drinks and he and Nora had a laugh about a cook they knew who had been chased out of town by a jealous husband.

We ordered hamburgers.

There was a particularly lively group at the end of the bar—three young men doing impressions of Barbra Streisand singing the national anthem.

Occasionally a tourist wandered in.

When we had just about finished our meal, a tremendous roar went up from a table near the front. I assumed that some celebrity had entered the bar. I craned my neck to get a look.

The girl who was causing the ruckus was an absolute stranger to me. She was young and rather pretty with a wealth of lovely raven curls, dressed in jeans, T-shirt, and leather boots. She didn't look like the toast of the town to me, but then I was out of touch.

I looked over at Nora for a clue, but she only shrugged.

It was Gus who filled us in: *that*, he said, was a newly crowned millionairess. "She's Bobbi Ann Budd." We were looking at the young dancer who was named executor of Peter Nestleton Krispus's will; she controlled "the millions left to those two lucky cats of his."

Nora and I pulled our chairs closer together and watched as Miss Budd took a seat at the bar. Her friends gathered around her, clapping her on the back, teasing, laughing, buying drinks, toasting her good fortune.

At one point, Gus gathered the big gray warrior of a bar cat up in his arms and plopped him into Bobbi Ann's lap.

"Do him a favor, hey, Bobbi Ann? Take him to live with the rich cats. At least give him a job as butler."

"Not a chance," she said, laughing. "Freddy boy is too old and beat up for that. Sorry, but he's just not our sort. What would they say at the cat country club?"

Insulted, the grizzled old cat roared his unhappiness. He took a swipe at Bobbi Ann Budd and then dashed away into the kitchen.

The crowd engulfed Bobbi Ann once more. We could hear no further conversation.

We were ready to call for the check, but when Nora raised her hand to signal our waitress, I grabbed her wrist and pulled it violently back down to the table.

"What is it?" she asked, alarmed.

"I just spotted someone!" I whispered. "I don't want him to notice us . . . me, anyway."

"Who is it?"

"Luther Kaminecki. Look over there—at

the table against the wall. He's mighty interested in Miss Budd."

I had no idea when he had arrived. He might have been sitting there all the time.

"Wow!" Nora said. "Okay, don't turn around. I'm watching him. He's just finishing his drink. I think he's about to leave . . . Yes, he's leaving. What are we going to do?"

"I'm going to follow him. You keep an eye on the young celebrity."

"Okay. Where do we rendezvous?"

"Right here."

"Should I try to interrogate her?"

I couldn't help smiling. Nora was really getting into it.

"Absolutely not, Nora. Just watch. Do nothing."

"But what if she leaves?"

"Let her."

Luther Kaminecki walked fairly briskly, purposefully.

I was surprised when he reached his destination: a music store.

Nothing so grand scale as Tower Records, mind you, and nothing so steeped in the atmosphere of the popular music aficionado as Footlight Records or Colony. No, this was simply a modest-size shop on 8th Avenue, crowded with old 45s and stacked floor to ceiling with CDs and cassettes.

I bought a coffee at the McDonald's across the street from the record store and found a spot in the window.

Oh, Lord! It must have been some little kid's birthday. Ronald McDonald was in residence today. The children surrounding him kept up a steady, astonishing din. What if Luther is a real browser? I thought. What if I have to stay here all afternoon while he's looking for some obscure record in that shop? I'll go mad.

Luther Kaminecki emerged from the music store about fifteen minutes later. It looked as if he had made no purchase. At least, I couldn't see a shopping bag, or a bag of any kind. His hands were still completely free.

His next stop was a Laundromat on 9th Avenue. Picking up the family wash for the Krispus clan? Why not? They tended to treat him like a retainer of sorts.

Or maybe it was his own wash. I didn't know where Luther himself lived. It would make a kind of sense if he, too, were a resident of Hell's Kitchen, which was the heart of the theater district. It would mean that he had lived close by his old idol, Peter Nelson Krispus.

But Luther wasn't picking up the laundry. Ten minutes or so later, when he walked out of the Laundromat, he was still empty-handed.

Stop number three was a nondescript little food market between 9th and 10th avenues—a *bodega*, in New York Latino parlance.

He didn't do any shopping there either.

Curious. He was either the world's pickiest shopper or the world's most compulsive neighborhood gossip—dropping in at local establishments to find what had transpired in the neighborhood during his absence.

Could he have lady friends in each of the stores he had visited and left empty-handed? But what sort of romantic visits took only ten minutes?

Well, Luther Kaminecki's final stop made all those other questions pale in comparison.

His last chat of the afternoon took place on a street corner—at 54th and 10th.

Luther stood there nervously waiting for a minute, and was soon joined by a toweringly tall lady-of-the-evening type with a shock of wiry, bright orange hair, backless pumps, and skin-tight Lycra pants.

Only it wasn't evening; it was daytime. And the lady was no lady; she was clearly a man!

The two of them talked quietly, if animatedly, for five minutes and then went their separate ways.

Luther must have been tired out by his schedule, because after that, he caught the first taxi he saw and zipped up 10th Avenue and out of my sight.

He'd put in a good afternoon's work visiting and I'd put in a good afternoon's work spying on him.

I didn't know what he had accomplished. But I had learned very little. All I'd done was confuse matters more, in fact.

Certainly, following Luther Kaminecki had not answered any of the questions that Nora and I had posed earlier.

I hurried back to Cozy on foot.

Bobbi Ann Budd was gone.

According to my operative's report—my operative being Nora—a young man, probably a boyfriend, had come in a short time ago, shared a drink with Bobbi Ann, and then whisked her off.

"Good work, Nora," I said encouragingly.

"What work? I couldn't hear what they were saying. And you told me not to approach her."

"That's right. We have plenty of time to hone in on Miss Budd and her part in the case."

Case? What a silly word to use. Was Nora's Sam Spade routine getting to me? John Cerise was not a "case."

"Young Miss Budd is rich now, isn't she?" I added. "She won't be going anywhere. Why should she?"

"Aha. Well, I guess that's why you're the boss," she said.

Gus knew how to make a decent negroni, too. He brought me one, and as I drank it I filled Nora in on Luther Kaminecki's strange stops all around the neighborhood.

The later it got, the more crowded the bar became. The customers were happily, rowdily singing along with every number on the inexhaustible tape of show tunes.

I tried to picture John Cerise here in this crowd . . . joking and camping with the other "kids." It wasn't easy to visualize.

Nora was in her glory, telling me the titles of the shows and reminiscing about the great stars she had worked with.

Suddenly the room fell quiet.

They were playing something sad now.

I asked Nora what it was.

She laughed wryly. "It's a song you ought to get to know, Alice."

"What is it?" I said.

" 'Send in the Clowns.' "

Chapter 11

What a frightening sound that was!

I sprang out of bed.

Yes, it was a frightening sound. But I knew I wasn't in any danger. I knew exactly what it was.

Bushy was choking and retching. Again.

I turned on the kitchen light and quickly found his medicine in the refrigerator. The vet had given me a six-month supply of the strange-smelling liquid that I had to feed poor Bushy, using an eye dropper, whenever he had one of these attacks.

Don't be alarmed, the vet had said. It's nothing out of the ordinary. Older cats suffer from a variety of stomach ailments. He might also start to lose his hair, have bowel problems, not see as sharply as he once did. It was all "to be expected."

The medicine calmed Bushy. A few minutes of pitiful mewling, and then he was back to normal.

I picked him up and held him tightly in my arms. "There you are, old sport," I said, kissing him on the head. "You're just fine now, aren't you?"

His contented purring told me that he was indeed fine.

"You're still my big beauty, aren't you?" I crooned. "Yes . . . You will always be my handsome young man. No matter how old you are."

It went through me then—like a thunderbolt. A memory, an image.

I suddenly saw in my mind's eye two startlingly beautiful young Maine coons sitting at the foot of their ailing master's bed. The cats who had inherited the mysterious Krispus fortune. George Bernard and Shaw.

What a silvery picture they made.

What's wrong with this picture?

That old expression went round and round in my head.

Everything! I realized. Everything.

I released the snoozing Bushy and ran to the telephone.

Nora was asleep. Of course she was. It was very late.

I apologized for waking her and then

quickly went on to make my request: I needed my best operative to meet me bright and early tomorrow morning at Grand Central Station.

"What's going on, Alice? Oh! It's the case, isn't it? Something about John . . . or Krispus."

"Yes," I said. "It's the case."

"Just tell me when and where to meet you."

"That's exactly what I hoped you would say," I told her. "You're a good man, Effie."

There are more newspapers and magazines in the brightly lit shop on the mezzanine of Grand Central Station than I have ever seen assembled in one place before in my life.

Every title imaginable. On every conceivable subject. In all languages. From all the countries of the world. Magazines for skiing enthusiasts. Magazines for photographers. Magazines for gun collectors, cigar aficionados, body builders, interior decorators, poets, woodworkers, single parents—not to mention the innumerable porno publications and breathless movie star rags.

The ones I was interested in were about

cats. Specifically, about breeding and buying pedigree cats.

I bought every cat-related journal I could find—surprised at the number of them—and then Nora and I repaired to the coffee shop on Lexington Avenue.

We pored over the magazines. Under my instructions, Nora compiled a list of all the breeders whose advertisements at the back of each publication said that they offered silver tabby Maine coons for sale. There were seven such breeders in all.

I sat there for a while, drinking my coffee and looking pensively over Nora's handwritten list.

"Okay, Alice. I've been a dutiful operative, wouldn't you say? I think it's time you filled me in on what we're doing here."

"I will, Nora. Soon. But first we have two other stops to make."

"What stops are those?"

"The OAC office."

"Why? Did you forget something there?"

"You might say that. And, in fact, if any of the other office people are there, that is exactly what we will say."

"And what's the other stop?"

"A visit with Glenda the Good, that's what. We have to return the keys, don't we?"

It was still early—not even 8:00 A.M. There were no other OAC staff people around.

My mission only required a couple of minutes, anyway.

I went over to the same desk where I'd located the fund-raising letters and searched for the letterhead stationery that listed John Cerise and Merlin Krispus among the board members.

I found the sheet of paper quickly.

Then I took Nora's list of silver tabby breeders out of my handbag.

It took no more than a few seconds to find what I was looking for: One of the breeders on Nora's list—a Mr. Hal Porter—was also on the OAC board of directors.

There it was! The connection. The link.

My memory of Hal Porter's name on that letterhead had been a mere impression, so fleeting and vague that it could hardly be called a memory. But now here was the confirmation of it . . . the proof that it hadn't been only a dream, something I had invented.

I shook the list in triumph.

Nora watched me, confused.

I folded the letterhead and put it, along with the breeders list, in my bag.

Still Nora watched me, holding her tongue.

I picked up the tan-colored office phone and called Lenox Hill Hospital. Glenda had been released the previous day, I was told.

Next, I dialed Information to get her number at home.

Glenda Fuchs answered on the second ring.

"Hello, Glenda. This is Alice Nestleton. Are you feeling better?"

"Thank you, yes. I'm sore all over, but quite okay."

"Good. I was wondering if now was a convenient time to drop those keys at your apartment."

"I suppose so . . . sure. but I have an extra set, so don't go out of your way. Are you in the neighborhood?"

"Oh, it's no trouble," I said, not really answering her question. "I'll be there shortly. What's the exact address and apartment number?"

Even in the taxi uptown, I wouldn't lay things out for Nora. It was a little too soon. I still needed Glenda's story to tie up the loose ends.

So we talked about everything but the matter at hand. I got her talking about the progress she was making with her musical comedy. That was enough to fill up the time until we pulled up at the weathered old walk-up on Amsterdam Avenue.

Glenda buzzed us in to her first-floor apartment and walked toward us haltingly. She thanked us again for our help with the mailing.

She looked genuinely surprised when I asked if we could come inside for a few minutes to talk.

"Of course," she answered and showed us to chairs. "I'll make coffee," she offered.

"No, that's all right," I said. "Don't trouble with that."

There must have been something ominous in my tone, because both Glenda and Nora went very quiet, both looking expectantly at me.

"Glenda," I said, "I know you did good work with John Cerise at OAC—work you should both be congratulated for. But now it's time to talk about the other part of your relationship with John."

Glenda was abashed, but she wasn't doing any maidenly blushing. She knew what I meant, I could tell.

"You *do* understand what I mean, don't you?" I said.

She had had a minute to gather her defenses by then. "I certainly do not, Alice.

Stop this mysterious fencing and tell me what you mean."

"All right, I will. Are you a big reader, Glenda?"

"Me? No, not particularly. I don't have much time for reading."

"Pity. There's an old O. Henry story that I'm sure you would find interesting. You'd relate to it, as they say. I think they even made a film of it long ago."

"What story?"

"It's called 'The Last Leaf.' It's about a young girl who lives with her sister in Greenwich Village. The young girls falls very ill and even the doctor thinks that she's going to die, mostly because she's lost her will to live.

"But the girl's enterprising sister and the old artist who is their neighbor cook up a scheme to give her courage.

"They tell her to look out of her bedroom window and take a lesson from a single leaf that is clinging to the vine against the fence outdoors. It's a lesson about fighting for life, about hanging on through the storm, no matter how hard it is. As long as the leaf stays, she can hang on to life, you see.

"And sure enough, the lone leaf manages to stay there through the cold, snowy winter. And when spring arrives, it's still alive and so is the girl. Alive and well again.

"The only thing is, the actual leaf had died months ago. The one that the young girl has been watching for inspiration was painted there by the old artist.

"The girl never knew that the leaf wasn't real—see? And they all live happily ever after."

Glenda sat motionless through my recitation. "What an inspiring story," she said ruefully when I was done. "Is there a point to it?"

I saw the same question in Nora's bemused gaze.

"I think there is a point for you, Glenda—a parallel to real life. And I think you know what it is. Isn't the scheme that you and John and a cat breeder named Hal Porter cooked up just a variation on that theme?"

Nora looked at Glenda. "Well?" she asked impatiently, even though Nora had no idea what scheme I was referring to. "Isn't it?"

I was waiting for the answer, too.

Glenda Fuchs took her time, but finally said quietly, "Yes. I suppose it is."

"So do I," I said. "You and John and Mr. Porter were replacing Peter Nelson Krispus's cats as they grew old, weren't you? Old . . . or sick.

"Krispus never even noticed. He was too ill

and too deranged to realize that he was growing old, dying, but his beautiful silver tabbies were not.

"I don't know whether it was out of kindness or for some other reason, but John was making sure that Krispus's pets would never grow old, never die. It was as if they were frozen in time.

"And you were helping him—abetting him—in the scheme. You and John acquired the new cats through this Hal Porter.

"The deception continued throughout Krispus's long illness. But before he died, his wife Adda must have learned about the will. She found out that Krispus was sitting on millions of dollars . . . and planned to leave it all to two cats.

"What's more, she knew that John was the one responsible for replacing the cats over the years. She had to have approved it. But now she blamed what she considered her husband's insane plan to leave the money to the cats on John. Perhaps she had just found out about the will on the night that Tony and I showed up for the party. At any rate, she held John responsible, and in a rage she killed him.

"That's what happened, isn't it, Glenda? That is why John died."

Glenda began to cry then.

"Yes," she said through the tears. "Yes, that must be why she did it. But . . . who knew things would turn out that way? Who knew he had all that money . . . and that he was going to cut his family out of the will and leave it to those cats?

"It *was* . . . insane. Krispus must have been insane to do something like that. But, don't you see? John thought he was helping the old man. He paid Hal Porter out of his own pocket . . . don't you see?

"And when the old cats were taken away, he found homes for them, or paid for their boarding until they died. He was like that. He was so fond of cats, and so fond of Krispus. But he didn't . . . I mean, how could he know how things would turn out? How could any of us know?

"When I heard that Adda Krispus had murdered John, I didn't know what to think. And then . . . then . . . when the story came out about the will, I was beside myself. I was partly to blame, I guess. I thought I was helping him. But I ended up helping him to get killed.

"My God, you can't imagine how terrible it made me feel. How guilty."

I allowed her to dry her eyes a bit before I went on.

"So the other members of the Krispus family knew what John was doing? They knew that he was substituting the cats?"

"I don't know," Glenda said, shaking her head. "I suppose they must have. Surely Adda did—and she must have told her sons. Were they blind? They knew but they never contributed to the scheme."

I didn't like to leave Glenda Fuchs crying, but there was no sign that she was going to stop crying any time soon.

Nora and I walked for blocks before either of us spoke.

We had reached the subway island splitting Broadway at 72nd Street by the time Nora said, "It is an insane story, Alice. But I think she's telling the truth. It all hangs together."

"That happens," I said.

"There's only one question I have now."

"I know."

"Yes. I know you know. Why did John refuse to acknowledge that he was John Cerise that night?"

"All I say is—as complicated as John seems to have been—I still don't know the half of his story. And now, I don't think I ever will."

Chapter 12

It was Aaron Stoner's day off.

He told me so when he phoned early that morning.

If I wouldn't have dinner, would I consider lunch? And if not lunch, would I at least take a walk with him? It would help him unwind.

A couple of days had passed since Glenda Fuchs admitted her part in the events leading up to John's death.

Stoner knew a great little cafe where they made coffee the right way—almost as good as the coffee in New Orleans.

I've never been to New Orleans. I said okay.

He picked me up at the loft and we began to stroll leisurely uptown on Hudson, then across town on 10th Street, and up 5th Avenue.

He was easy to be with—much easier than I would have predicted. Occasionally he took my arm, usually at the busier intersections, where we boldly crossed on red if there was no oncoming traffic. I thought only native New Yorkers did that, but it seems everybody enjoys flouting that particular law.

Lieutenant Stoner told me, somewhere around 11th Street, that he had confronted Adda Krispus with the replacement cat scenario, which Nora had passed on to him the evening we learned of it.

Adda neither confirmed nor denied that the switching of the cats—and the discovery of the terms of her husband's will—had been her motive for murdering John Cerise.

She remained as silent as ever about the whole incident.

"That was some piece of police work," Aaron complimented me. "It all sounds screwy as hell to me, but you scored, Miss Alice."

"Thank you. I just wish I could finish the puzzle . . . know for sure. John's behavior that night is still an unanswered question."

"Yeah, you find a lot of those in homicide work," he said philosophically. "Anyway, it's my guess that Adda Krispus will go to her grave without ever telling anybody the whole story."

I hoped that wasn't true. I didn't like the idea of never knowing why John had behaved as he had. But I had to admit it was a distinct possibility that I never would know all John's secrets.

At 14th Street we turned east and walked over to the farmer's market in Union Square. We picked up some luscious red grapes to nibble on as we walked, and Aaron bought me a sweet bouquet of dried flowers.

The coffee was fine at his special cafe, which turned out to be on University Place. We sat out on the little sidewalk portion of the cafe and drank café au laits from big white bowls.

"I may have to cut our visit short," I told him at last. "I've got a job to do in a few minutes."

"What job is that? I thought Nora said you weren't doing much acting these days."

"No, not that. I have to look in on a cat. I think I told you about that part of my life."

"Oh, right," he said. "Where is the little devil?"

"Not far. The apartment's in one of those huge, deluxe buildings across the park—

Zeckendorf Towers." I pointed toward one of the towers.

We could see the gold pyramid domes of the high-rises from our seats in the cafe.

"Why don't I come with you? I promise not to get in the way."

I hesitated with my answer, suddenly nervous.

For a minute I felt like a teenage babysitter worried about being caught at the neighbors' house with her Saturday night date.

But then I recovered.

"Okay. You can come—if you like cats."

"Why not?" Aaron said. "If you like 'em, I like 'em."

Barbarella was happy to see me. Aaron, she wasn't so sure about. She was just this side of rude to him, in fact.

I piled my client's mail in a basket on the bookshelf near the bedroom. Then I fed Barbarella and changed her litter box.

I let Aaron refill the catnip ball that Barbarella liked to play with. That broke the ice with her. She was all over him.

We outdid ourselves trying to find new ways to amuse Barbarella. Aaron had her laid out on the high-polished wood floor, playing a game he called "spin the cat."

"You'd better be careful, Aaron," I warned. "They can tire of a game like that pretty easily. And then . . . watch out."

In a while, the two of us stepped out onto the terrace, which was covered in thick ivy. Multicolored begonias at the peak of their loveliness surrounded us in their clay pots. We stood there in silence for a long while, looking at the city.

"It's beautiful up here, isn't it?" I finally said.

"Oh, it definitely is."

He was looking right at me, not out at the thrilling cityscape.

We were silent for another minute.

I felt very good in his company. I liked him a lot, but there were no specifics. I mean, I knew what I liked about Tony: He was handsome. He was intuitive. He was passionate—about me and about the theater. But this Stoner . . . well . . . perhaps it was the feeling I had that he was wise in a way I myself wanted to be wise.

"It's almost one," I said. "Are you getting hungry, Aaron?"

He went on looking at me, smiled, and shook his head very slowly.

I turned away from his gaze then, suddenly shy.

"Let's go inside, shall we?" I suggested.

"Okay."

But he didn't move.

Neither did I.

He was still looking at me.

"You're going to kiss me, aren't you, Aaron?"

"I'm going to try," he said and laughed. "Are you going to let me?"

"I think probably yes."

The kiss lasted for some time. When it was over I was the one smiling.

And then there was another kiss. An even deeper one this time.

He was still holding on to my waist when that one finally came to an end.

I made my good-bye to Barbarella a fairly hasty one. I thought it best that we get out of that comfortable apartment as soon as possible.

"Ask me again if I'm getting hungry," Aaron said as we rode down in the elevator.

"Not on your life," I replied.

The fact is, we were both ready for lunch. We decided to go to Pal Joey's.

Nora beamed at us proudly when we walked in . . . proudly, and a bit mischievously.

After she settled us into a booth and

poured a glass of white wine for each of us, she disappeared into the kitchen, promising to make us "a scampi to die for."

Aaron sat very close to me, his leg only a whisper away from mine under the white tablecloth.

"You got a nice appetite, girl," he commented as I went through my salad *frisée*. "I like that in a woman."

"Good," I said, tearing off another piece of baguette.

"You ever eat any crawfish?"

"No. What is it?"

"You'll see. Friend of mine flies it up here once in a while from down home. I'm going to fix you crawfish *étouffée* one of these nights."

I didn't say anything. And not just because I was eating. Aaron Stoner seemed to be getting a little sure of himself . . . or of me. As if he knew I wouldn't turn down a dinner invitation at his place. I didn't exactly like that. But at the same time, I didn't want him to think I would turn him down.

It dawned on me that he was old enough to remember the word "courtship." And I was old enough to appreciate it.

"Have you ever been married, Alice?"

"Uh-huh. Next question."

He chuckled. "Enough said."

He took the wine bottle out of its cooler and refilled our glasses.

"I was, too," he said.

"Married, you mean."

"Yes."

"Where is the ex Mrs. Stoner?"

"Back in New Orleans. She moved back down there after the divorce."

He anticipated my next question.

"Eight years ago," he said.

I didn't have to voice the question after that, either.

"When it was good, it was very very good, and when it was bad . . . well, that's why they make divorces, isn't it?"

We drank the creamy wine steadily, greedily, while I told him about my stalled acting career and how I came to be a professional cat-sitter and amateur investigator.

I was recounting the harrowing story of how Tony and I were almost killed one night when we were on a case in the Village.

Suddenly Aaron put his hand on mine briefly to interrupt my narrative.

"Tony is the guy you came into the station with that night, isn't he?"

"Yes," I answered.

"Him, in other words," Aaron said.

I looked up then.

Basillio was standing at the bar, staring at us, the veritable steam pouring from his ears and the proverbial daggers in his eyes.

It was instinct: I straightened my back and moved a couple of inches apart from Aaron.

I had done nothing to be guilty about, but Lord, did I feel guilty. And trapped.

"So this is the new hangout," Tony said when he reached our table. "Glad to see you're not at home pining away, Swede."

"Hello, Tony," I said quietly. "How are you?"

"Just swell."

"Tony, this is Aaron Stoner, as you probably remember."

"How *could* I forget? Enchanted, Lieutenant, as usual." He smiled cryptically at Aaron.

"How's it going, Cap?" Aaron said, his friendliness every bit as false as Tony's.

" 'Cap'?" Basillio repeated, mocking Aaron's accent. "What is that, anyway—a quaint southernism? You're up north now, friend . . . or should I say, 'boy'?"

Aaron merely laughed indulgently.

"Will you join us, Tony?" I asked, feeling miserable, and sounding it. I'm sure.

"No thanks," he spat out. "This isn't a pleasure trip—believe me. I'm here on business."

"What business?"

"It looks like you're going to be my landlord for a while longer," Tony said. "I haven't found another place yet. And anyway, why should I let old personal stuff drive me out of a perfectly good apartment before I'm good and ready to go?"

"No reason at all," I said. "Look, Tony, why don't you sit—"

"I said no thanks!"

He reached into his pocket then and flung two checks onto the table.

"Here's my rent for the next two months, landlord. *I've* got a job . . . in the theater . . . my profession, you know . . . unlike some other lazy people I could name."

"Tony, you should take it easy," Aaron said calmly.

"That's 'Take it easy, *Mr.* Basillio.' I don't go for civil servants calling me by my first name, cop."

"Really, Tony!" I said, indignant now. "You are being ridiculous."

"No more ridiculous than you and Gomer Pyle here," he said, sneering. "I'll leave you to your good ol' boy now, landlord."

"All right, Basillio, you do that. Do anything you like. As long as you get out of here and bring this childish scene to an end. Please."

Tony marched out without a backward glance.

Nora had witnessed the whole thing.

She was standing a few feet away, two plates of shrimp scampi in her hands.

"Wow!" was all she said.

Aaron began to say something to me—no doubt something soothing—but I hushed him with my hand.

"Well," I said when the plates were before us, "that was nice and mortifying, wasn't it?"

"That was delicious, Nora," I said.

I suppose it was delicious. I didn't pay much attention to my food. But I was damned if I was going to let Basillio's tantrum ruin my day. And I sure wasn't going to run after him.

"Fantastic scampi," said Aaron.

"Thanks, both of you," Nora said. "That bus-and-truck production of A Streetcar Named Expire wasn't bad, either. Even if Marlon left the stage before he ripped his T-shirt."

"Yes, that was quite a performance Tony put on, wasn't it?" I agreed.

"Well, skip it," she said lightly. "Your spirits will pick up tonight."

I couldn't imagine what she meant. "Tonight? What's happening tonight?"

"My party . . . remember? I'm expecting you and Aaron and a dozen other people here for a cocktail party. So you can meet Vince, my collaborator on the musical."

"Oh, dear," I said. "I guess I had forgotten."

"No excuse now," she said hurriedly. "So why don't you two scoot out of here. Get into your glad rags and I'll see you at six."

"I've got my glad rags all laid out," Aaron said. "How about you, Alice?"

I sighed, and had to hope that Nora didn't hear me. I was in no mood for a party.

But what I said was, "See you tonight, Nora."

"Great! I really do have to run now," she said. "I'm getting cut by Antonio."

"Cut by who?" asked a startled Aaron.

"Antonio. He has a new salon up on Madison. And I've got an appointment. I want a fabulous new do."

"Bully for you, Nora," I said. "Do you have

enough time to make a stop on your way there?"

"Sure, I guess so. Where do you want me to stop?"

I took one of the two checks Tony had flung at me and endorsed it over to the Our Alley Cats Foundation.

"Give this to Glenda Fuchs, with my blessing. She must be feeling pretty low now. But I just don't have the heart to see her again."

Out on the sunny sidewalk, I tried lamely to apologize to Aaron for the embarrassment Tony had brought upon him.

"Don't," he said, brushing it off. "I'd much rather see you forget it than apologize for it."

"Not so easy," I said, "but I'll try."

"You do that. I like you better when you're smiling. Like you did back there at Barbarella's."

I obliged him with a smile.

The best thing in the world, I thought, would be for me to go home and take a nap with the cats before I have to dress for the party.

Yet I remained on the sidewalk, returning that dizzy look that Aaron was giving me.

"I should get a cab," I said.

"No you shouldn't," he said.

Lydia Adamson

"I really should," I said.

"Unh-unh."

"Why not?" I said.

"Because," he said, "I have a car."

More than four hours later, Nora did *not* have a new haircut.

Even from the doorway of the bistro, as Aaron and I made our way across the room, it was plain that no ritzy coiffeur had had any part in Nora's "do," as she called it. It looked exactly the same as when we left her this afternoon.

There was something different about her, though. She was pasty as biscuit dough.

All in all, she looked just awful.

"Where have you two been?" she screeched as she rushed toward us, shoving the other partygoers out of her path.

I fumbled for words, and finally muttered: "I was napping . . . with the phone off the hook."

Aaron got a firm grip on her arm, steadying her. And she needed steadying.

"Nora, what is it?" he asked.

"I called you at the station, I called you at home," she said accusingly to Aaron. "I couldn't find you!"

"What is it, Nora!" I demanded, frightened. "What's happened?"

"It's that woman—Glenda Fuchs," she choked out. "I knocked on the door . . . It was open . . . No one there . . . I waited . . . waited . . . And then I tried the . . . the ladies' room."

A bistro waiter passed by then. I quickly plucked a drink from his tray and pressed it into Nora's hands.

"Go on," I said when she had taken a gulp. "What happened in the ladies' room?"

"Plenty," Nora said, "but it was all over by the time I got there. Oh, Alice, she's dead!"

"Dead? But I thought the doctors told her she'd be fine."

"It has nothing to do with any doctor," Nora said gravely. "She was murdered. Stabbed. To death."

Chapter 13

Nora was still kind of shaky. Like a housecat who encounters a malevolent canine for the first time.

She had followed Aaron's instructions last night, she said, and had gotten a good night's sleep.

I didn't quite believe her. There were deep circles under her eyes.

Even though she seemed to be coming back to life, I thought it best to stay close by her. So I was spending the day with her at Pal Joey.

Luckily, the lunch trade was very light. We sat around most of the afternoon drinking coffee, talking, and playing Scrabble.

Aaron came in to the bistro about two o'clock. He had just spoken to some of his colleagues on the homicide squad about the Glenda Fuchs murder and he knew we would want to hear the latest—within the limits of the NYPD confidentiality rules, that is.

The police theory was that Glenda had been killed in the course of a botched robbery.

"Now, how did I know you were going to say that?" I said cynically.

"ESP?" he replied.

"Not exactly," I said. "Nothing that out of the ordinary. It's just that you—I mean, the police—tend to go into a situation looking for a particular thing, and when they find it, it's all over for them. They light on the most obvious explanation for things, the statistical center. And it often takes a stick of dynamite to move you—them—off that spot."

Aaron's response to my tirade was admirably restrained. "You're saying you think she was hit then. You don't believe there was a robbery at all."

"If there was a robbery, so be it. But that wasn't the reason Glenda Fuchs was murdered. I know that as surely as I know it would be pointless, at this time, to try to convince your colleagues of that."

He nodded. "Well, we can be a little thick sometimes, can't we?"

I couldn't be sure whether he was genuinely offended. Somehow, I didn't think so. At any rate, I felt a surge of resentment at his tone.

"Don't take it personally, Aaron," Nora said, being conciliatory. "All Alice means is . . . well, you know how us private dicks are. We're always a step ahead of you cops."

Nora's words brought me up short. I became a little embarrassed, in fact. She had seen one too many old Warner Brothers movies. And maybe I was coming on just a bit too strong.

"I meant no such thing, Aaron," I said. "I'm sorry if it sounded like that."

"That's okay," he said, and I was relieved to see he was laughing. "I know you've got your own way of doing things, Alice. You're an independent thinker."

"I don't know how independent I am. It just amazes me that no one at Homicide is paying any attention to the fact that Glenda was nearly run down by a car last week. That was obviously the first attempt on her life."

He shrugged. "Maybe. But, by the way, as long as we're talking about people involved in your friend John's life . . . and death . . . I've got some other scuttlebutt for you."

Nora and I both reacted instantly.

"What?" I said.

Aaron poured coffee for himself as he talked. He had that astonishing ability to relax at anything he was doing.

"Looks like the tax people are interested in that will that Krispus left."

"You mean the IRS is after Bobbi Ann Budd already?" Nora said. "Even before the court fight with the rest of the Krispus people?"

"Not her," Aaron said. "The late Mr. Krispus. And all the rest of his family. They want to know if the old man reported all that income. They also want to know if the survivors are sitting on more hidden assets."

"Why not?" I mused. "Those people are good at hiding things."

"That's not all," Aaron nodded, that look of amusement reappearing on his face.

"Just don't tell us somebody else has been murdered," Nora said.

"What else?" I said.

"A judge has issued an order giving Bobbi Ann Budd immediate custody of those two cats. She got a lawyer to convince the court that it might not be exactly safe for the millionaire kitties to remain with the embittered Krispus sons—they could end up as pillow stuffing or something."

"I don't think that's so funny, Aaron," I said harshly. "She may be be right."

He sobered then.

"Okay. Enough kidding around. Listen, Alice—and you, too, Nora. That Krispus family might be nuts. But they could also be dangerous. One of them is already locked up for murder, remember.

"And as for the Fuchs woman—maybe she was killed in the course of a mugging and maybe she wasn't—maybe it was a hit—I don't know. But if you're right, if she *was* hit, that's all the more reason for the two of you to back off and let the cops handle things."

"I've heard that before, too, Aaron," I said wearily. He sounded like Tony. Or my ex-husband. Or several other men I could think of. They were always warning me about something or other. What is it with men? Where does that obsession with warning come from?

"It's good advice," he snapped.

He softened a second later, though. "The cops aren't your enemies, Alice . . . certainly I'm not."

"I know," I said. Yes I knew. Still, he was starting to obscure the issue.

"So don't do anything crazy, okay?"

"Yes."

"Nora," he said, turning to her, "I'm counting on you to rat her out if she does try anything crazy."

"What am I—the stool pigeon?" Nora asked.

"I've got to go back to work, ladies. See you."

When Aaron was gone, Nora looked intently at me.

"Well, Alice," she said, "are you going to drop it now? Is the caper over for us?"

"You know the answer to that, Nora," I said quietly. "The *case* is just beginning."

"I know Aaron's a bit of a chauvinist, Alice. But he's right about not doing anything too dangerous."

"Oh no. Don't worry about that. I'm not about to tangle with any murderers just now. When I say 'the case,' I mean John Cerise's real story—his past. John's kind of a missing person now. And I've got to find him."

"We," Nora corrected me. "We've got to find him."

At the bar, a man was tinkling the ice

cubes in his glass. Oddly, the sound cut through the chatter in the room.

My neck tensed suddenly. I began to knead it. This would be my second and last hunt for the real John Cerise. The first one had ended with the benign revelation that my friend had been a Broadway hoofer in his youth. This one would have to do better. There wouldn't be a third.

As my grandmother used to say, cryptically, "Never comb a devil with no hair."

Chapter 14

"Alice I've got to hand it to you."

"What?" I asked in reply to Nora's remark.

"You took me to a place I've never been before."

"Good," I said. "I'm glad. Let's just hope we've come to the *right* place."

Actually, there was no chance that we were lost—no, nothing like that.

I just meant that I hoped we would find what we were looking for. There was no other place to go.

We were in the reading room of the Performing Arts Library of Lincoln Center.

Laid out before us on the long table we had commandeered were stacks of theater annuals and old *Playbill*s, dating back almost forty years.

We were looking for Broadway musicals— famous ones, obscure ones, lavish ones, modest ones—in which John Cerise might have appeared as a chorus line dancer.

For each play, we knew we could skip right over the list of major cast members and go straight to the bottom of the program, to the small print, where the names of the standbys, dancers, chorus members, and understudies appeared.

Starting about 1958, John's name began to turn up with regularity.

"What's this one?" I asked, handing a program to Nora.

She identified the show immediately. "*Wildcat*," she said. "You know, Lucille Ball . . . oh, that's right. You don't know anything. You're a Broadway ignoramus."

"Here's another one—*Holly*, it's called. What was that one about? A Christmas show?"

Nora took the program from my hand. "Oh my goodness. This was a legendary failure. A one-night disaster. Right up there with *Kelly*."

"Right up there with what?"

"Never mind. *Holly*, to answer your question, was a musical based on *Breakfast at Tiffany's*."

"You're joking."

"Nope. Richard Chamberlain and Mary Tyler Moore were the stars."

I was speechless. I didn't get musicals at all.

We went on searching. We were in a kind of frenzy.

Nora was floored when she discovered John's name listed in a short-lived musical—*Rio Nights*—in which she herself had appeared, in 1961.

"Oh, my God! Look at this, will you?" She was pointing at the cover of the *Playbill*, which showed a caricature of the two stars of the show kissing. In the background was a drawing of Nora wearing an outlandish headdress.

"Is that *you*?" I asked, almost gushing, like a starstruck yokel.

"If you think that one is bad, take a look at this," she giggled.

I read the name of the show: *The Tender Typist*. Nora was pictured in a short skirt, hair bobbed, legs crossed, looking very much like a Shirley MacLaine clone.

"Pathetic, isn't it?" she said self-effacingly.

"It is not. You were cute as a button," I said, borrowing a phrase from my grandmother. "And look here at the cast list."

"Don't tell me John was in that one, too!"

"No," I said, "but look at the list of girl dancers. Look!"

She followed my finger on the page.

"Letty Ann Budd," she read out loud. "Budd? Budd! As in—"

"As in Bobbi Ann Budd," I finished her sentence triumphantly. "The young dancer who's executor for the Krispus will. Let's go back over some of the other cast lists where John's name appears. See if Letty Ann Budd's name is on any of them."

That was the key, it turned out. John Cerise and Letty Ann Budd appeared six times in the same shows. Always in the chorus line or in minor roles.

"I think we have enough to go on, Nora," I said an hour or so later. "I've got another assignment for you now."

Less than twenty-four hours later, Nora had carried out part one of the assignment. Namely, she was able to call on enough old theater contacts to confirm that Bobbi Ann Budd was indeed the daughter of Letty Ann Budd, the former Broadway dancer.

I was sure that Nora would be able to carry out the second part of her assignment as well: getting me an interview with Letty Ann.

I was eager, to say the least, to speak to Letty Ann Budd. There were a hundred questions I wanted to ask her—about John, about her daughter, about Peter Nelson Krispus, and all the threads connecting the parties of this case.

Unhappily, that turned out to be impossible. Letty Ann had retired years ago. And in 1989 she died of breast cancer.

So, my hopes of uncovering some of John's secrets through Bobbi Ann Budd's mother also had to be buried. That route was closed to me.

As for young Ms. Budd's father . . . well, he was dead, too. But I already knew that. After all, his death was what had started the whole investigation.

I didn't have any birth certificate before me. I hadn't yet looked up any hospital records, or located the obstetrician or the attending midwife. But I knew with absolute certainty that John Cerise was the father of Letty Ann Budd's child.

It just couldn't be any other way.

My heart—and my head—told me so.

It also told me that this one ray of light on a gruesome double murder had entered through a fast-closing door. I had to push it open—now!

Chapter 15

Nora looked as if she were off to a midnight picnic.

She removed item after item from her totebag, which was like the horn of plenty. She had brought white wine, red wine, roast chicken, marinated artichokes, tuna salad, white asparagus, green salad, French bread, lemon tarts, chocolate cookies, and a couple of stray delicacies I couldn't even identify.

"You didn't have to do all this, Nora," I said. "I could have taken care of dinner."

"No problem, sweetie," she answered. "I know you can't cook."

I hadn't exactly said I *couldn't* cook; I had merely told her that I *didn't* cook very often. But I let it pass.

We set up everything on the kitchen table. The lovely, savory aromas filling the room were intoxicating.

I thought the cats would lose their minds.

Bushy growled so pathetically that Nora sliced a bit of chicken and handed it down to him.

Pancho received his portion and immediately made off with it, as though it were his own secret mouse.

"What a cute place you have, Alice," Nora said, looking around the loft. "But why are you living over here in no-man's-land? Don't you fall into the Hudson every time you get out of bed?"

"It's a very long story, Nora. I'm a little isolated, living so far west, but I love it. And God knows, it's cheap."

Over dinner, we talked about the scandalous scene Tony had pulled at the bistro. I hadn't heard from him since.

Nora also wanted to talk about me and Aaron Stoner. I kept pushing the conversation in other directions. But, while we were still at the table, the telephone rang and my answering machine took the call.

Aaron.

He was leaving a message that was beginning to veer into the strictly personal.

I hurried over to the machine and turned the volume all the way down.

When I turned back to Nora, there was a mile-wide Cheshire cat grin on her mouth.

"That's my girl," she said.

"I'll make coffee," I said, ignoring her remark.

"Don't bother. In the thermos."

"You mean you even brought coffee?"

"Yes. I was afraid you'd only have that nasty instant. I'm very particular, as you must have guessed by now."

"All right, Nora. We've dined royally. Now it's time for work."

We took our coffee into the living room— or what I called the living room—that area of the loft containing the sofa and a couple of flea market armchairs, a coffee table, and half a dozen cat toys.

Perhaps "work" was the wrong word to have used. Perhaps I should have said it was time for my lecture.

I didn't set out to be pedantic, but I knew myself—knew that when I got to this point in the case, I acted a bit like a puffed-up old professor. I paced. I gestured foolishly. I thought aloud. I fired dozens of seemingly unanswerable questions into the air. And sometimes proposed the answers to them— some answers were logical, some fanciful. Whoever was in the room with me became my student body, my captive audience, my sounding board. Tonight, Nora was it.

"What we have here, Nora, is not so much a coherent scenario, one fact or event following another, as a set of curious, puzzling events and actions. They're random. Crazy, even.

"And what we have to do is put them all together and tease some kind of sense out of them.

"Let me start to list the elements . . . in no particular order."

"And I'll hold all my questions till the end of the lecture. Is that how it works?" Nora asked.

"Yes. Pretty much," I said.

She settled back on the sofa and tucked her legs in. "Okay. Ready."

"Number One," I began. "The puzzle that began everything. John Cerise encounters me in the Kripus apartment. I know who he is as well as I know my own name. But he denies being John Cerise.

"It was a classic case of being caught with your hand in the cookie jar. John looked terribly embarrassed—no, that isn't even the word. Not embarrassed—guilty. Now, what was he so guilty about?

"He had to be doing something dishonest, something underhanded.

"And I know it wasn't because of the cat-switching trick. That isn't something he'd feel the slightest bit of guilt about.

"Perplexing Fact Number Two: It is now established that at least one member of the Krispus family other than Peter Nelson Krispus knew John Cerise—that person being Merlin Krispus. And it is very likely that all the other family members knew John. Yet they all deny it. Why?

"Perplexing Fact Number Three: Peter Nelson Krispus was supposed to be broke. Yet he had more than two million dollars. Where did it come from?

"Perplexing Fact Number Four: It cannot be a coincidence that the young girl who was named executor of Peter Nelson Kripus's will is the daughter of the man who engineered the cat-replacement scheme—the same man who was murdered by Adda Krispus.

"So what kind of connection between John Cerise and Kripus would be powerful enough to make Kripus leave two million dollars in the care of John's child?

"Number Five: What is the meaning of the empty cassette cases we found in John's apartment? What was he doing with all those soundtracks from kiddie movies? And who would bother to take them? In other words, who posed as John's brother?

"Number Six: What was Luther Kaminecki doing that day? Why did he make those apparently pointless stops—the music store, the laundry, the deli, the transvestite hooker. What ties him to all those people and places?

"And, in turn, what ties those people and places to Peter Nelson Krispus or John Cerise?

Number Seven: It is obvious that Glenda Fuch's hit-and-run accident was no accident. Someone made two attempts on her life. The second succeeded. Who wanted her dead? What did she know that was so threatening to that person?"

Nora waited a moment, making sure that I had finished. Then she gave me a round of applause.

"So," she said, "now you're going to give me the answers, right?"

"Not exactly, no. Not to everything, anyway. But here's something else to factor in:

"Wherever that two million came from, it was definitely dirty. And the Krispus family knew it. We don't know whether they helped

Krispus get it, but they knew it was dirty. They were simply waiting around to inherit it.

"Then, when the bombshell dropped that the money was not being left to them, Adda went crazy."

"And you don't have a clue where the money came from?" Nora asked in dismay.

"A clue," I repeated. "I wouldn't say I don't have a clue, Nora."

I went silent for a long time. Nora did nothing to break my concentration.

I may have been silent, but my mind wasn't. It was racing, alive with fragments of conversations, remembered expressions on various faces, sights, sounds. A chaotic operetta playing itself out behind my eyes.

Since I had discovered Bobbi Ann Budd's paternity, a simple line of logic kept popping into my head. It was the logic of greed and larceny. I wanted something grander . . . more exotic. I hate it that people die for money. Die for love or honor or beauty. But not money. Alas, it was the only game in town.

At last, I spoke again. "Nora, I think we're not so far away from answering a lot of those questions."

"What do you mean? You've solved the case?" she said, incredulous.

"Maybe. It all depends on—let's say it partly depends on you."

"*Me? How?*"

"Well, it's only fair to tell you that . . . if you agree to help me . . . you'd be putting yourself at risk. Would you be willing to do that?"

Nora folded her arms. "I knew it!" she declared.

"Knew what?"

"I knew when Aaron told you not to do anything crazy that it wouldn't be long before you'd be doing something crazy."

"Oh, that," I said, somewhat abashed. "But this isn't crazy. It's a risk, as I said. But I hardly think it's crazy to try to solve this case. To try to put John's memory to rest. To try to get some kind of justice for Glenda Fuchs and her alley cats. What I can't do is demand that you put yourself in the way of trouble."

"Oh, skip it," Nora said impatiently. "Of course I'll help you. The good guys never get hurt too bad, right? And we're the good guys. Our hearts are pure—right?"

"Pure as Ivory Snow."

"Just what are you planning to do, Alice? And when?"

"Tomorrow," I said decisively. "Tomorrow

we bait the trap . . . and then . . . snap it shut."

I brought my fist down hard on the coffee table.

"Ouch!" she said, wincing. "Who's going to get caught in this trap?"

"Nora, that isn't our problem."

Chapter 16

Nora's Sam Spade/pulp fiction references were a constant source of amusement for me. I am a far cry from a whisky-drinking, ironfisted film noir hero. And even Nora herself was only half serious about the hard-boiled detective bit.

But that day, I had to admit I was falling into a sort of Raymond Chandler mood. Before I left that afternoon, I put on a hat.

Eighth Avenue in the rain.

"Are we all set?" I asked Nora.

"All set," she answered solemnly.

We were standing in a kind of grassless park where many people who worked in the area ate their lunch or sat out sunning on nice days—a landscaped public space provided by the office building across from the McDonald's where I'd been trapped at the children's birthday party.

Tailing Luther Kaminecki that day, I watched him go first into the music store across the avenue. That was where the operation Nora and I were engaged in would start.

I decided that I should go in first and check things out. If I don't come back within five minutes, I told Nora, proceed with the plan.

I crossed the street and went in to the shop. I was a bit scared.

The man behind the counter had a balding pate and a long ponytail. He wore an Irish fisherman's sweater.

Sitting at a cluttered desk against the far wall was a much younger man in a denim shirt and jeans. He was filing index cards in a box. He took absolutely no notice of me, but then I realized that he was wearing earphones. Lost in his rhythmic swaying and filing, I don't think he would have noticed if Arnold Schwartzenegger had come in.

I got a brief look at the tape he was listening to when he removed it from his Walkman and flipped it over: *West Side Story*.

When the long-haired man behind the raised counter asked if he could help me I shook my head lazily.

"I'm just browsing," I said. "I'll let you know if I need help."

I strolled around the room for a while and then came to rest a few feet away from the cash register, pretending to be engrossed in a stack of Birgit Nilsson records.

Nora came in six minutes later, shaking the rain from her umbrella.

She didn't wait for the man to ask if she needed assistance. Instead she walked directly up to the counter, and after taking a preliminary look around the place, leaned in toward him.

"Are you the owner here?" she asked.

"Yes, I am. Is something wrong?"

Rather than answering the question, she forged ahead: "Do you buy as well as sell?"

"That depends," he said. "If you have anything that looks interesting. We sometimes buy entire collections."

"Excellent, excellent," said Nora, "because I have quite an extensive collection of tapes. And I'm looking to get a good price for it . . . a *very* good price."

The owner said nothing in reply to that. He looked curiously at Nora.

"I understand you specialize in certain . . . certain kinds of music," Nora continued.

"That's right. What were you thinking of selling—opera? jazz?"

"Not exactly," Nora answered. "To be honest, I think children might enjoy these tapes more than adults."

Her voice had dropped to just above a whisper.

That had exactly the effect she meant it to have. It just made the man lean closer.

"Actually," she said, "I have a great number of copies of the same cassette."

I could almost feel the tension in the man's neck. I picked up one of the records I was fiddling with and walked over to a different bin with it in my hand, feigning a complete lack of interest in their conversation.

"What cassette?" I heard him ask, his voice low.

"*Dumbo*," she answered slowly.

The owner's eyes darted around the room once.

"I also have *Snow White*," Nora added, her voice back up to normal volume now.

The man in the sweater pulled back suddenly.

"No thanks," he said.

"No thanks to what?" Nora asked, managing to sound menacing.

"Everything," the owner said coldly. "We're not interested."

"Are you sure about that?" she said with a mysterious smile.

He turned his back on Nora then. "I'm very busy here," he said, picking through some useless papers near the register.

Nora made a quick exit.

I heard the shop door slam shut. The sound sent a bit of a shiver up my back, but I tried not to react.

The shop owner glanced my way, and all he saw, I hoped, was a quirky music fan in an old fedora, comparing recordings of *Madama Butterfly*.

He picked up the receiver of the black rotary telephone then.

Were I a little animal, my ears might have gone up like antennae.

But all I heard was the sound of the receiver being settled back in its cradle.

"Miss, are you nearly finished?" he called over to me.

I pretended not to hear, forcing him to call out again, "Miss, are you going to be much longer?"

"Well, I . . . I'm almost—"

"I'm sorry, but you'll have to come back

later this afternoon. I'm closing up for lunch."

"Are you really?" I said imperiously. "How European."

And with that, I placed the Birgit Nilsson record in the wrong bin and breezed out.

Ponytail wasn't going anywhere for lunch. I heard him dialing even as the door closed behind me.

Nora and I met up under the marquee of the movie house on 50th Street, between 8th and 9th avenues.

As planned, she was carrying a laundry bag filled with soiled old tableclothes and napkins from the bistro. She had stashed it with the movie house usher before our music store act.

I congratulated her on the good work she did with the music store owner. Then we stepped out into the rain once again, heading for the Laundromat around the corner, Luther Kaminecki's second stop.

Not too many people doing laundry. The weather was keeping them away. That was good.

Who Am I This Time? I once saw a rather charming play with that title. It was about a group of actors in an amateur theater troupe.

This time, I was a difficult—maybe deranged—customer who was furious that the Laundromat didn't sell my favorite brand of detergent. I made an enormous stink with the manager, a portly man of about fifty with a pencil mustache. I griped about everything—the size of the driers, the fact that there was no soda machine, the outrageous 75-cents-per-load prices.

He finally walked away from me in disgust and returned to the counter where the cash register and the scales for weighing bags of laundry were located.

I busied myself first with finding a free washer and second with locating a comfortable place to sit and doze while my things were in the machine.

Of course, I wasn't actually dozing.

I settled myself into a chair near the counter where the manager stood.

Then in walked Nora in her tan raincoat—cocky and contentious.

"Who's in charge here?" Nora asked loudly of the thin woman who was folding clothes near the front of the laundry.

The woman pointed to the counter at the rear of the room.

Nora strode back there. She was smoking a cigarette. I could smell it as she passed by me.

"Hey, you!" she barked at the manager.

I guess the man was a little tired of over-bearing women by then. He stood with one hand on his hip.

"What the hell do you want?"

"I'm only going to say this once," Nora replied. "So listen good. I've got a shipment. Come up with the right figure and it's yours."

"Shipment?"

"That's right, buster."

He broke into derisive laughter at her use of the outdated slang. "A shipment of what, lady?"

"*Dumbo*, that's what. *Dumbo* and *Cinderella* and all their friends."

He stopped laughing. "What are you talking about?"

"I told you!" Nora said impatiently. "I'm not going to repeat myself. You're wasting my time here. Are you interested or not?"

He looked searchingly at the woman standing before him, legs apart, rain dripping steadily from her umbrella onto the linoleum floor.

"Who *are* you?"

"Never mind that," Nora snapped. "I know who you are. That's all that counts. Now, are you interested in the tapes, or do I go someplace else?"

He stood there, shaking his head. "Get out of here. I don't know what you're talking about. Get out of here."

Nora shrugged. "It's your funeral, buster."

She turned on her heel and in a few seconds she was gone.

The manager hurriedly slipped on his jacket. He exchanged a couple of words with the thin woman near the door, then left the Laundromat at a trot.

I followed.

He was running up the block, searching through his pants pockets as he went.

At the corner he stopped, unlocked a dark green Volvo, and in a matter of seconds was speeding away.

I had instructed Nora to go in search of the wiry-haired transvestite when the curtain fell on the Laundromat scene.

The next scene was all mine.

The trim man shelving canned soups at the bodega turned around when I walked in.

"Good afternoon," he said in greeting.

I smiled back at him.

He was arrestingly handsome, with silken black hair, shining ebony eyes, a dancer's hips and torso, and a tiny waist.

I didn't think he was anyone's idea of a typical grocery store clerk.

"Julio!" someone called to him from the back of the store.

"Yeah?"

"Delivery!" the disembodied voice answered.

"I'll be back," Julio promised and vanished into the rear of the store.

It gave me a few minutes to look around the deli, which was spotless. The stock was neatly arranged on the shelves, the floors were newly swabbed down, the marble counter was clean and uncluttered. Even the front window was spanking clean.

All in all, the bodega was a big change from the usual deli in this neighborhood, where more often than not the customer was buying cigarettes and cheap canned beer, and once in a while a lunchmeat sandwich.

Julio didn't just look like a dancer. He *was* one. Or had been, before he retired.

A couple of minutes of idle flirting while I plucked Oreos and cornflakes from the shelf elicited that information.

"Anything else I can help you with today, lovely senorita?" the gallant Julio asked me when I had amassed a little pile of groceries on the counter.

"You know, Julio, I'm so glad you asked that," I said. "You can help me a lot today, as it turns out."

"Oh yes?"

"Yes. You see, I'm a little short on money right now."

"Who isn't, my fair lady?" he said, the gleam in his eye already dimming.

"But that's just it, Julio. If we can do a little business today, there's money in it for both of us."

"*Both* of us, huh?" He laughed. "That's a new one on me, baby. What kind of scam are you into?"

"No scam," I said reassuringly. "Not at all. I've got something you may want to buy. And then you can sell it for an even higher price. You know, the usual way. That's what the system's all about, isn't it? Wholesale and retail. Supply and demand."

"What are you talking about, miss?"

"Tapes," I said, my voice hard, serious.

"You've come to the wrong place," he said, trying to brazen it out. "This is a grocery store, miss. We don't sell tapes."

"Oh yes you do, Julio. You do sell tapes—

for instance, *Snow White* and *Dumbo* and *Cinderella.*"

He looked stricken, ill. "Where did you—"

Julio stopped himself there.

"That's right," I said. "Better not to ask any questions. Now is it yes or no on the T-A-P-E-S?"

"It's N-O," he spat out.

"Suit yourself, Julio," I said. "See you around."

"Just a minute!" he shouted as I walked toward the door. "Who are you?"

"Who am I? My name is Nora Karroll," I called back. " 'Bye, Julio."

The trap was truly baited now.

Nora had played quite a few parts in her time, including two stellar performances today.

But now it looked as if she was being cast in the role of damsel in distress.

Just as I rounded the corner onto 10th Avenue, I saw her cowering before the orange-haired transvestite, who was raising her beaded handbag over Nora's head as if to strike her.

I screamed before the blow landed. The red head took off on her wobbly high heels.

I ran over to Nora. "Are you all right?" I asked, out of breath.

I couldn't tell whether she was laughing or crying. Maybe both.

It was still raining.

Back at Pal Joey Bistro, we sat with our cups of steaming hot tea. I was wolfing down the finger sandwiches that Nora's sous chef had made for us.

"Who'd have thunk it?" Nora observed wryly. "I start out to play Della Street and end up playing Edward G. Robinson."

"I did sort of wish I had a video camera for your scene in the Laundromat," I said. "The only thing missing was a cigar in your mouth."

She laughed. "I bet Robinson never got beaned with a drag queen's purse. Anyway, for your sake," she said resignedly, "I hope all your traps don't turn out this way."

"What do you mean?" I said.

"What do you mean, what do I mean? It was a bust, wasn't it? A failure. I didn't hear any trap clanging shut."

"Of course not," I said gently. "That's because it hasn't been sprung yet."

Her eyes widened. "Oh my God, you mean there's something else?"

"Yes," I said. "There's something else."

"More risks to be taken?"

"Right. But actually we weren't really taking any risks with those four characters today—beaded bags notwithstanding.

"You see, all those guys are just prosperous businessmen. Or, should I say, part of a prosperous business. We weren't in any real danger from any of them."

"So where does the real risk come in?" Nora asked. "When does the trap really slam shut?"

"Tonight, most likely," I said. "Tonight. Right here at old Pal Joey."

"We should both go home and change out of these icky, damp clothes," Nora said.

"Sorry," I said, "but that's a no-no."

"A no-no? Why's that?"

"Because, Nora, for the rest of the day, you and I have got to keep a very low profile. As a matter of fact, we have to disappear."

"Oh," she said, and then, after skipping a beat, asked, "Why?"

"You'll see in a minute," I said. "First, let me double check something with you: Pal Joey closes at midnight tonight, is that correct?"

"Yes."

"And your whatchamacallit—you know, your right-hand person in the kitchen . . . "

"The sous chef?"

"Right—she's on duty tonight?"

"Yes."

"Good. Because she's going to have to handle the dinner trade tonight. You won't be anywhere around. In fact, the whole staff should be told to say you're not in tonight if anyone should ask. Starting right now, you don't even answer the phone."

"Okay."

"And finally, I do want you to make one telephone call out. Just say exactly what I tell you to say."

"I hear and obey, boss."

She picked up one of the sandwiches and separated the two slices of bread.

"Slam!" Nora cried, banging the two slices together violently like the jaws of a steel trap clanging shut.

Chapter 17

From the noise out front, it sounded as if business was good that night.

But that was just a guess.

We couldn't know for sure because Nora and I, in our black waiter's pants and white overshirts, had been hiding in the office at the back of the restaurant all evening.

The staff was told to carry on as though Nora were home with a toothache.

The night sure passes slowly when you're confined in the dark. Unable to talk. Unable to make a sound. No playing Scrabble. No playing the radio. No nothing.

You find yourself wondering who's calling you at home now. What are the cats doing? How does the moonlight look from your window?

But the night did come to a close. Finally.

Finally, the digital clock on Nora's office desk read 12:00 A.M.

We could hear the clanging of pots in the kitchen; the busboy emptying the scrub pail; the scraping of chairs as they were set up on the tables for the night; the cash registers zinging as the day's receipts were added up.

And then the dying of the lights out front.

All quiet. All black.

Yes, the restaurant was closed now. But the truth was, it was more important than ever for us to be careful, to be silent.

Sure enough, not thirty minutes after the last muffled "good night, see you tomorrow" was said out front, we heard noises in the restaurant.

We both went rigid.

As Nora had pointed out many times, the Pal Joey Bistro did not have mice.

In another minute, the door to the office creaked open. I could hear Nora trying to suppress her breathing.

Quick, desperate footsteps.

An urgent whisper.

Our plan was to wait until the count of ten and then throw on the wall switch. The culprit or culprits would be caught off guard, pinned there in the light while Nora trained upon them the derringer that she kept in her desk drawer.

But the intruders upstaged us on that move. One of them went to the desk and snapped on the green-shaded lamp.

"That's right," I said calmly. "You know exactly where everything is . . . don't you, Gus?"

I flicked on the overhead lights.

"Sweet Mother Macree," Nora uttered. "Gus! You son of a . . . "

It was the friendly bartender from Cozy. The one who had so helpfully told us about Bobbi Ann Budd. The one I had Nora call earlier in the day, to ask if he wanted to make a few extra bucks waiting tables tonight at the bistro.

And standing next to him, paralyzed and staring as though hypnotized at the muzzle of Nora's gun, was Jane Krispus.

"I don't know how you were planning to get into the wall safe," I said to Gus. "But it wouldn't have done you any good, even if you had the combination. Because there aren't any tapes there . . . or anywhere else."

Gus and Jane remained wordless.

"You see what I meant about this being fairly low risk, don't you, Nora?" I said.

"These two don't exactly seem like Bonnie and Clyde to me."

We waited. The silence was deafening. Nora kept waving the silly gun. The air in the office had become suffocating.

"What if they never utter another goddamn word?" asked Nora.

"That will be fine," I said. "There isn't a lot Glenda Fuchs's murderers could have to say for themselves."

Jane Krispus cracked then.

"I didn't kill her!" she protested. "Neither did he."

"Oh really?" I said archly. "Are you sure that things didn't get out of hand . . . that even though you two didn't set out to kill anyone, you decided Glenda had to be silenced . . . because she knew too much?"

"No!" she insisted. "That was . . . "

"Go ahead, Jane," I said. "That was who? You'll have to tell the story soon anyway. Who did kill Glenda? It's him or you, Jane. Who did it?"

"Luther," Gus said tonelessly. "Luther Kaminecki."

Nora still had her pistol out, but I had allowed Jane and Gus to sit.

He was smoking greedily while Jane talked, and he would not meet Nora's eyes.

"It didn't start with us," Jane said, gesturing to include Gus. "None of it started with us.

"Long ago, my father-in-law—before he was my father-in-law—hit upon a scheme that would bring in thousands of dollars. It had to do with the kind of Broadway musicals that he despised. The ones he worked his whole life to undermine. He couldn't stand the idea that he was nothing more than a fringe figure, no more than a fly-speck in theater history, while those shows that he hated so much were beloved by millions.

"So his scheme was to exploit those shows—and the people who mounted them—and the people who revered them—for his own ends.

"He had partners in the scheme. People who were at the very heart of the musical theater tradition. The most important were two dancers. John Cerise and Letty Anne Budd.

"Eventually Gus became part of it. And of course Luther Kaminecki. Eventually even I got on the gravy train. But at the beginning it was Peter, John, and Letty Ann.

"What, Peter asked himself, do the real die-hard fans of Broadway really want, other than the show itself? Answer: They want everything. They want to know the stars. Warts and all. They want to know how a Broadway show is put together. They want all the juicy gossip. They want to know who's sleeping with who. All sorts of things like that. The dirtiest linen behind the sweetest songs.

"So, Letty and John became his spies. They wore hidden wires during the latter stages of any show they appeared in. They captured the frantic last-minute changes. The all-important dress rehearsals. And they sometimes bugged their coworkers' dressing rooms.

"Pretty soon, there was enough insider material to delight any Broadway groupie. It was a way for fans to hear numbers that didn't make the final cut of a show, who got fired in New Haven, who the director's girl-friend was, who was secretly gay—every-thing.

"You'd be surprised how many big-time shows were involved. John and Letty were essential parts of the shows—but totally un-heralded. Nobody knew their names . . . and surely nobody suspected them of anything.

"As the years went by, other performers had to be recruited. Younger singers or dancers who could be trusted to get the good stuff on tape. And who could be trusted to keep their mouths shut."

She stopped talking for a moment and looked over at Gus, as if asking for support. Gus did not respond. When she resumed the story, she spoke more slowly.

"The distribution of the tapes got to be a bit baroque, but it was a tight-knit group of discreet people. One ex-dancer bought a grocery store as a front. They mix tapes in his basement.

"Another conspirator ships from his music store midtown. And so on.

"Needless to say, the real names of the shows can't be bruited about, so a series of codes was worked out.

"Sometimes they use the names of animated features. You know, *Cinderella* could really be *Sunset Boulevard*; *Dumbo* might be the *Showboat* revival.

"Some other labels are innocuous 'how-to' titles: something like *How to Repair Your Bathroom Faucet* might be *Les Misérables* . . . whatever.

"Hits. Flops. Shows that closed out of

town. It doesn't matter to the Broadway fanatic. All that matters is being in the know.

"Peter would sometimes recruit a producer's assistant or a costume mistress. Or a sound effects man who needed money. All kinds of people with an entree into that world and a bit of larceny in their hearts. People like Gus, for example, who worked as a stage manager for years.

"Just imagine, at $200 to $500 a tape, for all those years, Peter had a better investment than municipal bonds.

"And Peter *needed* money, if he was to go on in his odious ways. He was quite the seducer, you know. He had a string of women over the years. And he kept most of them in fine style. All the while flaunting it in Adda's face, poor devoted dog that she was.

"Then of course he had to help bankroll his own productions. One failure after another. One arcane extravaganza after another. You must see how that could eat into his bank account."

I stopped her there.

"All right, Jane. You've said why Peter Nelson Krispus needed money. What about John and Letty? How could they do something so despicable?"

"Why do you think they did it?" she said

impatiently. "Poverty is a pretty good motive, don't you think? That, and simple human avarice. How did John support his lifestyle—on his savings from a career as a chorus boy? Not likely. How do you suppose he became a feline dandy? Where do you think the money for his home in New Jersey came from—wealthy parents? No. John was like me—never really had anything when he was young. He figured it was high time to get something out of this world."

I took a minute to let that sink in. This was the first time I accepted as truth some bad motive ascribed to John Cerise. It didn't hurt like I expected it to.

I wanted Jane Krispus to go on with the story, of which there was bound to be plenty more.

"What about the rest of the Krispus family?" I asked. "What about your husband? Did they know about Peter's business? Did Adda?"

"It's complicated, the answer to that question," she said. "The answer is no—and yes."

"They were beginning to realize that Peter had amassed a lot of money. He was even beginning to dispense little bits of it to them here and there—being magnanimous in his old age. He funded Merlin's antique busi-

Lydia Adamson

ness last year, and offered to send Hume and me away on a cruise earlier this year. I guess that old bastard knew he was dying and wanted to make up a little for being such an awful father.

"So, yes, they knew there was money. But they weren't aware of how he came by it. All they knew was that he was bound to die soon, and they were his rightful heirs. Little did they know," Jane added with a bitter laugh, "that their inheritance was ear-marked for two cats!

"They didn't find out about the tapes until recently—just in the last year. Around the same time my husband discovered I was having an affair . . . with John. It was after John took the apartment in the city that he learned what was going on between us."

My!

That wrinkle took me by surprise. But I wasn't unhappy to hear it. I was glad that John had had someone in his life, and it was becoming increasingly clear that Jane had really loved him.

"I'm not a bit sorry for it," she said defiantly. "I made an awful marriage with Hume and I couldn't get out of it. It felt as if I were married to all of them—all those soul-killing people name Krispus—and I grew to detest them all. Still, I just didn't know how to walk away from it. John was helping me to do just that. You see, I planned to leave Hume and he knew it."

"Do you think Hume told Adda that, too?" I asked.

"Very likely, yes."

Oh, I thought. Yes, that makes sense. Another reason for Adda's murderous rage at John. Another nail in John's coffin.

"Jane, do you know Bobbi Ann Budd?"

"Yes," she answered warily.

"She is John's daughter, isn't she?"

"Yes."

"Is she a nice girl?" I asked wistfully. "Were she and John close?"

"She's a wonderful girl, Miss Nestleton. And no, she had no part in any of the shenanigans. John loved that girl and would have done anything to keep her out of trouble. You must believe that."

"All right. I believe it."

"And yes, she and John were close, as you say. But he—he never even told her she was his child. She knew him only as an old friend of her mother's. He was Uncle John, who helped her whenever she needed a friend. I had just convinced him to tell her the truth. After we moved in together, after we . . . married . . . he was going to tell her the truth."

Jane was crying softly, staring straight ahead.

The truth. What a simple word. It was in fact anything but simple in this case.

"Tell me about Luther Kaminecki now," I said after Jane had had a few minutes to collect herself.

"He's a lecherous old—"

She broke off there. "Oh, what's the use in putting all the blame on Luther? He didn't do anything worse than the rest of us—not at first anyway.

"But he was convinced that John was telling Glenda Fuchs about the tape scam. I don't know why. Perhaps he thought John was going soft. Luther had the nerve to . . . disapprove . . . when he heard about our affair. I know he didn't like it that John included me in the profits. And he was always afraid that after Peter's death John might quit rather than allow Luther to run things.

"Luther was a frightened man. But he didn't have to kill that woman. John hadn't told her a thing."

"At any rate, Luther confessed what he'd done to Gus. He said he was acting to protect the whole group, and if he was ever caught, arrested, he'd take us all down with him—tell the police that we all decided to kill Glenda Fuchs."

Jane looked pleadingly from me to Nora and then back to me. "We didn't know what Luther was planning, Miss Nestleton. I swear to you, we had nothing to do with Glenda's death. We're not killers, any of us. It was just a matter of . . . of . . ."

"Poverty? Human avarice?" I filled in wryly.

Jane fell silent.

"I'm sorry, Nora," Gus said, barely audible.

Nora merely shook her head.

"Julio and the others were freaking out today," he said. "And when I heard that you—you, of all people—were trying to cut in on our action . . . maybe even blackmail us . . . well, I had to see what you had in here."

Nora stared at him blankly. "But how did you know—" she began.

"That doesn't matter right now, Nora," I interrupted. "I'll explain it later. Right now, we have to call the police. I'll try to get Aaron Stoner. He'll be quite happy to see what a better mousetrap can do."

"Thank God," Nora said. "I thought I might have to use this thing."

She waved the pistol around carelessly.

Alarmed, Gus ducked.

He needn't have. I knew there were no bullets in it.

Chapter 18

I was somewhere in that strange zone between waking and sleeping.

That time when you have the saddest
dreams.

In this one, Nora is giving a glamorous
party in a Manhattan penthouse worthy of
an old William Powell movie. All the guests
are dressed in glittery evening wear and
tuxedos. The talk is witty and sexy and
knowing, and the champagne is flowing.

A man with pearly white teeth is playing
show tunes on a baby grand with keys that
sparkle in the same way his teeth do.

In the midst of all the flirting and gaiety, I
float through the room with a mournful expression on my face. I am wearing a long
dress made of ostrich feathers.

Suddenly there is a tremendous commo-
tion over by the French doors. One of the

women guests is so frightened that she faints.

I see framed in the door to the balcony a hulking dark bird who is flapping his wings desperately against the glass. In a furor, he begins to throw himself against the French doors.

Everyone else is running away in terror from the huge bird with its eyes like liquid fire. I alone go toward him—floating to the window as if being pulled by an invisible string.

I can see the bird clearly now.

He caws. He cries. He flails.

We are face to face now, the angry bird on his side of the glass, I on mine.

I can see his anguish. I try speaking soothing words to the creature. But he does not understand.

At last, his tortured bird sounds turn to screams—human screams—and the bird is no longer a feathered creature but a man in a shabby coat.

He is Tony Basillio.

I pry the French doors open then, and reach for Tony, both arms out.

But it is too late.

He tumbles backward over the railing and disappears, blending into the black night.

I got up and made a cup of tea and sat in the early-morning light drinking it, shivering, scared.

The cats stirred for a few moments, looking around to see what was happening. Satisfied that all was well, they retreated to their respective snoozing spots and fell off again.

Enough loss, I found myself thinking. Enough dying. Enough mourning.

Later in the morning, when the rest of the world was up, I called Basillio.

He wasn't very friendly at first. But he didn't hang up.

He liked his new job, he said. But then, it was always great to be working with young people. The members of this energetic and talented theater troupe looked upon him as a kind of wise old veteran. And, surprisingly, that felt good—even when one of the beautiful young actresses was clearly talking to him as if he were her grandfather.

I caught him up on my life. And I told him about the outcome of the John Cerise/Krispus mystery. He was suitably impressed and complimentary about the way I had solved the case.

We said maybe we should have dinner some time next week—maybe. And we left it at that.

Not a word was spoken about Aaron Stoner. Tony didn't mention him and neither did I.

"Say hi to Nora for me, will you?" he asked at the end of the conversation.

I assured him that I would.

"And the thug, too," he added.

"Who?"

"Pancho," Tony explained. "Say hi to Pancho, too. I kind of miss him."

It seemed the conversation was over.

But he didn't hang up.

Neither did I.

Pancho zoomed past me, too fast for me to pass on Tony's regards to him.

I waited.

"Swede, I want to say something."

"Say it."

"I am worried about you."

For some reason, I found that line to be funny. I laughed out loud.

"I think maybe you've lost your way."

That was even funnier. Pancho came scrambling by again. Bushy climbed onto my lap.

"I mean," Tony went on, "about the theater, Swede."

"Sure, the theater," I repeated.

"What I'm saying, Alice, is that you're spreading your talents too thin."

"Aren't we all?"

"I mean all this crime nonsense . . . all this cat-sitting stuff . . . they're taking their toll."

"I act when I can, Tony. What the hell do you want me to do? Go back to drama school productions of one-act early Tennessee Williams?"

Again there was a long silence.

"Swede . . . for people like you and me, that's all there is."

"Maybe you should go back to sleep, Tony."

"Wait!"

"I'm waiting."

"Do you remember what Brecht said?"

"About what?"

"About Broadway."

"No."

"He said it was merely on insignificant aspect of the international drug trade."

"That's ridiculous."

"He didn't mean it concretely. It was a metaphor."

"I loathe metaphors."

"He meant that you have to get rid of every infatuation. There's the actor, the audience, the script, and what happens between them. That's all."

"But, Tony," I said wildly, wickedly, "I'm just a little farm girl from Minnesota. That's all I have—infatuations."

"Obviously you're not interested in having a serious conversation."

"Actually, Tony, I'd like to have a serious conversation—with Marlene."

"You've lost me."

"Dietrich. When I was eighteen everybody said I was sort of a milkmaid version of Lola Lola in *The Blue Angel*. And don't you remember her song '*What Am I Bid for My Apples*'?"

Silence again. Then I heard a whiskey bottle being opened.

Pancho jumped up on the window ledge and arched his back in an attack stance.

"That's all people like you and I have," Tony whispered. "The theater."

Then he hung up.

"No," I said into the dead receiver. "I have a lot more."

Then I walked over to Pancho.

"Do you remember John?" I asked.

Pancho didn't answer.

"He said you were the reincarnation of one of Napoleon's marshals."

Pancho wasn't impressed.

"I don't know what to do, Panch. I don't know who to trust."

He stared at me.

"I mean, Pancho, your friend John is dead and you friend Tony is gone."

Suddenly I felt an insane fury toward Tony. Who the hell was he to question my allegiance to the theater!

Then it abated.

This, too, shall pass, I thought.

"Tony says hello to you, Panch."

And then I started to clean the house.

Chapter 19

To our delight, Nora was running frantically around the perimeter of the loft rustling her long wool skirt and giving out with exaggerated cries of "Oooh la la!"

She was parodying one of the dance numbers from *Can-Can*.

She ended with a modified Moulin Rouge-type split that sent Bushy howling into the bathroom.

Aaron Stoner, Nora, and I did some howling of our own. I couldn't remember laughing that hard in years.

When we all calmed down a bit, I opened the special bottle of wine Nora had brought.

Aaron had brought a present, too. He gave me four Swedish wine glasses. I guess it was his diplomatic way of saying that my thick, industrial-looking water tumblers were unsuitable for any liquid that cost more than $3.99 a bottle.

The sudden quieting of the mood seemed to turn all our thoughts toward the serious and maybe even tragic aspects of the case—cases—we'd all been involved in.

It was strange. You couldn't exactly say we had all worked together on the case; it just felt that way.

I became involved because of John Cerise and my refusal to accept his terrible death at face value.

Should I have accepted it? I found myself wondering. Would it have been better to let things alone? I would never have learned that he was—to be blunt—a criminal, a crook. I would never have been pulled into the tangled, pathetic lives of the Krispuses, not to speak of the very unattractive Luther Kaminecki.

But of course I would never have known that John had left a child behind. No matter what, that couldn't be a bad thing. I hoped I would get the chance to get to know Bobbi Ann Budd one day. The last I heard, she was planning to provide the Our Alley Cats group with a generous endowment.

Nora Karroll had realized her dream of playing Della Street. And then some! I could not have managed the investigation without her. In fact, I'd worked with policemen, professionals, who weren't half as intuitive or resourceful or sharp as Nora.

She had had the time of her life helping me crack the case, she said, but for now she was trading in her raincoat and gun for her stained white apron and deboning knife. She had to get back to her real profession—restaurateur.

As for Aaron, maybe the facts of the John Cerise/Krispus case were eccentric—"loony," he even called them—but it was all in a day's work for him. He dealt with murder, greed, lies practically every day. Had it not been for my part in things, and Nora's, it would have been just another case for him.

"They got Kaminecki just about nailed on the Fuchs murder," Aaron said. "That's even before all the larceny, copyright infringement, tax evasion, eavesdropping, diversion of funds, and kitchen sink charges that are going to come down on his head."

"When will that be?" I asked. "Haven't Jane Krispus and Gus confessed everything, signed a statement?"

"Yeah, they have. Well, let me put it this way: They've filled in the blanks. They gave us the whole history of the scam; outlined the distribution setup; told us where the storage was. The Feds have confiscated thousands of those cassettes. D.A. says he's preparing more than a dozen indictments."

"What haven't they told?" Nora said.

"Everything but the names of the individual dancers and singers. I don't know whether they really don't have the names, or whether—"

"Whether they're protecting the gypsies," Nora finished for him. "That would make sense. Put everyone behind bars. But let the gypsies go on to dance another day."

She was smiling a little.

"And what about Adda Krispus?" I asked. "Anything illuminating from her?"

Aaron shook his head. "She's still a piece of furniture. I can't see the judge sending her to prison, though. She'll probably end up at one of the laughing academies upstate. I hate to sound so brutal, but how long is she going to live anyway?"

"Yes, of course you're right, Aaron," I said pensively.

I was thinking of John at that moment. Not just about those horrible last few minutes of his life but about the whole sweep of it. Good and bad. High and low. It was as if

I'd been holding his hand all this time—holding the hand of a corpse—dragging him around with me—and now I could let go.

I looked over at Stoner. He seemed comfortable, at his ease in his powder blue cotton sweater.

But once in a while his eyes seemed to wander, as if he were thinking of some other place. Home? Was New Orleans still home, really? He was such an odd mix—a southern-born New York City cop with sophisticated tastes in a whole lot of areas. I trusted him.

"Aaron?"

"What?"

"Something is gnawing at me."

"What's that, *chérie*?" He looked at me flirtatiously over the rim of his wineglass.

"The reason why."

He laughed. "No one to this day knows the reason why the Light Brigade charged into the Valley of Death."

"I'm talking about why Peter Krispus left his money to Bobbi Ann Budd."

"Jane Krispus says she doesn't know why. But there aren't too many options, are there, Alice?"

"No. Not too many," I agreed. "It could have been just chance. She was around. He trusted nobody in his entourage to take care of his cats. So he made her the caretaker."

"Possible," he said.

"Or she really could have been the last in a line of young women that the old rake seduced."

"Possible."

"Or it could have been something else, Aaron. Something very ugly."

"More than possible, Alice. Probable."

I was silent for a long time.

"Well?" an impatient Nora asked.

"Let me do the honors," Aaron said gallantly. "John Cerise acted as a—well, shall we say, he made arrangements between his daughter and Krispus—put them together—so that the old man would leave her the money. It was Cerise's perverted legacy to the daughter he never really acknowledged and the woman who bore her."

It was the saddest horror story I'd ever heard.

I let go gently. But I did let go.

An hour later we were back in high spirits.

We were listening to a few of the bootleg cassettes that had managed to fall out of one of the crates in the Evidence Room at the station house.

"Here's one I'm really curious about," I said, picking up one of the cases. "Let's try this one out next."

Lettered on the spine of the plastic holder was *101 Dalmatians*.

I placed the tape in the tape deck. Before I could return to my seat, I heard the music from the overture swelling and dipping—triangles and horns and crashing cymbals.

"Oh, no," Nora groaned loudly. "Excuse me while I gag."

I looked over at Aaron, who was exaggeratedly rolling his eyes.

"What?" I asked the two of them. "What is it?"

"Alice," Nora said, "do you mean to say you don't recognize this music?"

I shook my head. "No. What is it?"

The two of them laughed at me—openly laughed at me—and then said in unison:

"*Cats*, Alice . . . *Cats!*"

Be sure to catch
the next
Alice Nestleton mystery,
A CAT ON THE COUCH
Coming to you from
Signet in November 1996

Chapter 1

I always seem to end up in strange places with strange cats.

It was six-thirty on a beautiful fall morning. I was sitting in a taxi that was hurtling north on 8th Avenue. Traffic was light and the cabby almost seemed to be flying up the avenue.

Next to me on the back seat was a carrier, and in the carrier was a cat named Roberta.

I had picked Roberta up at her very posh lower 5th Avenue domicile and was bringing her to an animal psychologist on Central Park West to get her dear little head straightened out.

How I ended up in that cab with that cat is not really a mystery.

My friend Nora Karroll, who owns a bistro called Pal Joey in the theater district, became friendly with one of her longtime bistro denizens, Joseph Vise.

Vise is one of those "almost famous" character actors. Everybody knows him but nobody knows his name. He is getting on in age now, and he alternates between playing lovable grandfathers and ruthless old Mafia dons.

He had been offered a small part in a TV movie that was shooting out of town and needed a cat-sitter for his lovely little short-haired tortoiseshell cat, named after his departed third wife, Roberta.

Nora had asked him what he was willing to pay. Vise responded with the magic words, "money is no object." Nora recommended me highly. He called me and the deal was made. All he told me was that once in a while little Roberta acted "peculiar."

"Peculiar, as in violent?" I asked warily. "You mean she bites? She claws? Hates strangers?"

"No, no," he said. "Nothing like that. She's just . . . peculiar."

My first visit to Roberta went just fine. She couldn't have been sweeter.

The second time was even better. She loved the paper airplanes I made for her and she even ate some of her dry food right out of my hand.

But the third session was a disaster.

I was just about to leave Vise's apartment when I saw Roberta glaring at me from inside the fireplace.

"Roberta!" I scolded, "you get out of there this minute!"

She strolled out, throwing a devilish look my way.

Then, in a single bound, she was up on the fireplace mantel. She reached out delicately with one paw and sent a framed photograph of one of Joseph Vise's ex-wives smashing to the hearth, glass flying every which way.

Next she ran into the bathroom and began crazily unraveling the toilet paper.

Eluding my grasp, Roberta raced back to the living room and viciously swatted a green glass vase filled with fresh flowers off the plant stand.

Then, suddenly spent, she lay down on her back, all four legs in the air, and promptly went to sleep.

I stood there in a kind of shock.

This was what "peculiar" meant to Joseph Vise?

He didn't seem surprised when I called

him in Toronto to report on the carnage. He merely assumed his Mafia godfather voice and said, "It is time to do something about Roberta. I warned her. She shows me no respect."

And that is how I ended up in that cab, that morning, with that cat.

I was taking her to her first session with the eminent animal psychologist Wilma Tedescu.

Mr. Vise had assured me that Mrs. Tedescu was very good—and, not incidentally, very expensive. The procedure she followed was this: the pet owner had to be interviewed once by her alone, and once along with the troubled feline. Vise had already gone through the two processes.

After the therapy commenced, Vise told me melodramatically, it would be Wilma and Roberta alone.

As to her treatment methods, they were not known to Vise, except that she relied heavily on playing with the cat in various ways and with various objects.

Now, I have no feelings one way or the other about animal psychologists. Or are they called feline therapists?

I did once read and thoroughly enjoy an impressive book by a canine therapist who used what she called the "secret language of dogs" to treat neurotic dogs in Hollywood very successfully.

In short, I maintained an open mind. And I was sympathetic with Joseph Vise's plight.

After all, I did have a borderline psychotic at home. Pancho, my old gray alley cat, spent his entire waking life fleeing from imaginary enemies. It was the consensus that Pancho was a nut. But I loved him like crazy.

Tony Basillio, my ex-boyfriend, once suggested a nutritional therapy for Pancho. "Give him," he said, "an unplucked chicken and a bowl of buttermilk every three days."

I didn't think it would work. Surely, not for Roberta.

My personal evaluation of Roberta was that she was regressing to some infantile state. She really seemed to enjoy knocking things over for no other reason than to hear them shatter.

Obviously, she needed help.

When the taxi reached our destination, I realized that Wilma Tedescu's dwelling was not on Central Park West itself. Just west of that avenue, it was a large, ill-kempt brownstone with treacherous, crumbling steps.

Up I trudged with Roberta's carrier in tow.

There was only one bell and one mailbox. It looked as though Wilma Tedescu owned the entire building.

I rang.

There was no answer.

I rang again.

Then a woman's voice boomed out through heavy static.

"Please state your name and your purpose," the voice said.

I realized it was a security check.

"My name is Alice Nestleton and I've brought Joseph Vise's cat Roberta for . . . "

I stopped there, stuck. It was too early in the morning. The only word I could think of was "therapy" and I was just too embarrassed to use it.

The bright fall wind started blowing my hair about. I thought of an acceptable synonym. "Treatment!" I blurted out triumphantly.

There was a pause.

"Please enter when you hear the buzzer and be seated."

"Yes, madame," I said under my breath, mocking the stentorian transmission.

The buzzer went off. I pushed through the heavy door, stepped inside, and let it bang shut behind me.

I had entered a hallway. At the end of it, I

could see a kitchen. To the left was a staircase. To the right was a sitting room with a
sofa, a few chairs, and a large magazine
rack. On the walls were prints of jungle
cats—jaguars, ocelots, civets.

I carried Roberta into the sitting room.

I heard muffled voices off somewhere.

On the other side of the room was a half-
open door.

Through it, I could see Wilma Tedescu's
profile. She was seated in a chair, talking to
someone I could not see . . . presumably a
person, not a cat.

I realized she was probably conducting
one of those interviews Joseph Vise had told
me about. And it was she who had activated
the intercom when I rang the outside bell.

Even in profile I could see that she was a
very large woman. I understood why Vise
had characterized her as a middle-aged
Valkyrie.

I looked at my watch. We were a few minutes early. I sat down on the sofa with the
carrier next to me.

"Be patient, Roberta," I counseled.

Roberta gave me one of those feline
groans that bubbles up from the stomach.

I sat back, trying not to eavesdrop but
catching disjointed parts of the conversation

going on in the office. Wilma Tedescu seemed to be doing all the talking. I couldn't make out exactly what she was saying . . . something about cats and furniture . . . but she had a very pleasant voice with a trace of a southern accent.

My thoughts went to poor Roberta, who was shifting about in her box.

"There's nothing to be frightened of, kid," I whispered. "No needles, no clippers, no pills, no X-rays. This is not a vet's office. Understand?"

She looked at me balefully.

"The nice lady is just going to talk to you . . . put some sense into you."

Roberta turned away from me dismissively.

"Don't be like that," I said. "You can't just go around knocking photographs off mantelpieces," I warned her. "It's just no way for a lady like you to behave."

Not when *I'm* cat-sitting for you, I thought.

I plucked a magazine out of the rack. It was an old *New Yorker*. I looked at the cartoons.

Then I studied the photographs of a carnival in Martinique in the *National Geographic*.

Then I read a recipe for Cajun coleslaw in *Redbook.*

Undoable! I had to chuckle at the image of myself attempting to prepare that dish.

Then I looked at my watch. It was five minutes past seven.

Another ten minutes passed. I started getting very agitated.

But the woman was still talking. Had she forgotten that we were there? Well, I wasn't going to let poor Roberta suffer anymore, so I opened up the carrier and peculiar little Roberta ambled out. Now, let's face facts. There is nothing on God's green earth as elegant as a cat stepping out of a carrier. There just isn't. Roberta shook herself a bit and then settled next to me on the couch.

By seven twenty-five I knew it was time to say something. I cautioned Roberta to cause no trouble, stood up, and walked to the door.

I heard all the magazines hit the floor, but I didn't bother to turn around to remonstrate with the cat.

I knocked at the office door, and when there was no answer I stuck my head in. "Excuse me."

Wilma Tedescu didn't turn around. In

fact, she paid no mind at all to the interruption.

Then, to my amazement, I realized that Wilma was completely alone in the room. The chair I had assumed was occupied by a client was absolutely empty.

And Wilma wasn't speaking. The words I had been listening to were coming from a tape recorder in the open top drawer of her desk.

I walked to the front of her chair so that I could face her foursquare. She still hadn't said a word.

It took about five seconds to realize that she never would. She was dead. There was a small, oh, ever so small trickle of blood coming from beneath her right ear . . . where the bullet had entered.

For some reason I called out: "Roberta, come in here."

And believe it or not, the little rascal ambled in.

Yes, the woman was a Valkyrie. I could see that clearly even as she sat dead in the chair. She was wearing a long blue dress with a small checked apron over it. Maybe her last thoughts had been about what to make for breakfast.

Excerpt from A Cat on the Couch

I didn't scream. I didn't panic. I just reached down into the drawer and turned off the recorder.

Then I picked Roberta up in my arms and hugged her.

Enter the mysterious
world of Alice Nestleton
in her
Lydia Adamson series . . .
by reading these other
purr-fect cat capers
from Signet

A CAT IN THE MANGER

Alice Nestleton, an off-off-Broadway ac-
tress-turned-amateur-sleuth, is crazy
about cats, particularly her Maine coon
Bushy and alley cat Pancho. Alice plans
to enjoy a merry little Christmas peace-
fully cat-sitting at a gorgeous Long Island estate where she expects to be
greeted by eight howling Himalayans. Instead, she stumbles across a grisly
corpse. Alice has unwittingly become
part of a deadly game of high-stakes
horse racing, sinister seduction, and
missing money. Alice knows she'll have
to count on her catlike instincts and
(she hopes!) nine lives to solve the murder mystery.

A CAT OF A DIFFERENT COLOR

Alice Nestleton returns home one evening after teaching her acting class at the New School to find a lovestruck student bearing a curious gift—a beautiful white Abyssinian-like cat. The next day, the student is murdered in a Manhattan bar and the rare cat is catnapped! Alice's feline curiosity prompts her to investigate. As the clues unfold, Alice is led into an underworld of smuggling, blackmail, and murder. Alice sets one of her famous traps to uncover a criminal operation that stretches from downtown Manhattan to South America to the center of New York's diamond district. Alice herself becomes the prey in a cat-and-mouse game before she finds the key to the mystery in a group of unusual cats with an exotic history.

A CAT IN WOLF'S CLOTHING

When two retired city workers are found slain in their apartment, the New York City police discover the same clue that has left them baffled in seventeen murder cases in the last fifteen years—all of the murder victims were cat owners, and a toy was left for each cat at the murder scene. After reaching one too many dead ends, the police decide to consult New York's cagiest crime-solving cat expert, Alice Nestleton. What appears to be the work of one psychotic, cat-loving murderer leads to a tangled web of intrigue as our heroine becomes convinced that the key to the crimes lies in the cats, which mysteriously vanish after the murders. The trail of clues takes Alice from the secretive small towns of the Adirondacks to the eerie caverns beneath Central Park, where she finds that sometimes cat-worship can lead to murder.

A CAT BY ANY OTHER NAME

A hot New York summer has Alice Nestleton taking a hiatus from the stage and joining a coterie of cat-lovers in cultivating a Manhattan herb garden. When one of the cozy group plunges to her death, Alice is stunned and grief-stricken by the apparent suicide of her close friend. But aided by her two cats, she soon smells a rat. And with the help of her own felinelike instincts, Alice unravels the trail of clues and sets a trap that leads her from the Brooklyn Botanic Gardens right to her own backyard. Could the victim's dearest friends have been her own worst enemies?

A CAT IN THE WINGS

Cats, Christmas, and crime converge when Alice Nestleton finds herself on the prowl for the murderer of a once-world-famous ballet dancer. Alice's close friend has been charged with the crime and it is up to Alice to seek the truth. From Manhattan's meanest streets to the elegant salons of wealthy art patrons, Alice is drawn into a dark and dangerous web of deception, until one very special cat brings Alice the clues she needs to track down the murderer of one of the most imaginative men the ballet world has ever known.

A CAT WITH A FIDDLE

Alice Nestleton's latest job requires her to drive a musician's cat up to rural Massachusetts. The actress, hurt by bad reviews of her latest play, looks forward to a long, restful weekend. But though the woods are beautiful and relaxing, Alice must share the artists' colony with a world-famous quartet beset by rivalries. Her peaceful vacation is shattered when the handsome lady-killer of a pianist turns up murdered. Alice may have a tin ear, but she also has a sharp eye for suspects and a nose for clues. Her investigations lead her from the scenic Berkshire Mountains to New York City, but it takes the clue of a rare breed of cats for Alice to piece together the puzzle. Alice has a good idea whodunit, but the local police won't listen so our intrepid cat-lady is soon baiting a dangerous trap for a killer.

A CAT IN A GLASS HOUSE

Alice Nestleton, after years in off-off-Broadway, sees stardom on the horizon at last. Her agent has sent her to a chic TriBeCa Chinese restaurant to land a movie part with an up-and-coming film producer. Instead, Alice finds herself right in the middle of cats, crime, and mayhem once again. Before she can place her order, she sees a beautiful red tabby mysteriously perched amid the glass decor of the restaurant . . . and three young thugs pulling out weapons to spray the restaurant with bullets. A waitress is killed, and Alice is certain the cat is missing, too. Teamed up with a handsome, Mandarin-speaking cop, Alice is convinced the missing cat and the murder are related, and she sets out to prove it.

A CAT WITH NO REGRETS

Alice Nestleton is on her way to stardom! Seated aboard a private jet en route to Marseilles, with her cats Bushy and Pancho beside her, she eagerly anticipates her first starring role in a feature film. To her further delight, the producer, Dorothy Dodd, has brought her three beautiful Abyssinian cats along. But on arrival in France, tragedy strikes. Before Alice's horrified eyes, the van driven by Dorothy Dodd goes out of control and crashes, killing the producer immediately. As the cast and crew scramble to keep their film project alive, Alice has an additional worry: what will happen to Dorothy's cats? As additional corpses turn up to mar the beautiful Provençal countryside, Alice becomes convinced the suspicious deaths and the valuable cats are related. She sets one of her famous traps to solve the mystery.

A CAT ON THE CUTTING EDGE

What do you do if your beloved kitty suddenly becomes a snarling, hissing tiger when you try to coax him into his carrier for a routine trip to the vet? If you're savvy cat-sitting sleuth Alice Nestleton, you call for help from the Village Cat People, a service for cat owners with problem pets. Yet Pancho's unruliness becomes the least of Alice's worries when her Cat People representative, Martha, is found dead at Alice's front door. Martha's friends sense foul play and ask Alice to investigate. Alice would much rather focus her attention on her new loft apartment in twisty, historic Greenwich Village. But a second murder involving the Cat People gives her "paws." When a series of clues leads Alice to a Bohemian poet and trendy New York's colorful past, the Village becomes the perfect place to catch a killer.

A CAT ON A WINNING STREAK

Out-of-work actress Alice Nestleton is willing to go as far as Atlantic City for a gig. Relaxing in a fabulous suite, she is startled by a slinky cat crawling up to her sixteenth-floor window. Alice's quest for its owner takes her to the nasty scene of Adele Houghton slashed to death, and her roommate, Carmella, standing there covered in blood. Naturally, the police nab Carmella, but her handsome lover insists she is innocent and begs Alice to find the real killer. Alice is ready to bet that the murderer did in poor Ms. Houghton in order to steal her legendary, dice-charming cat. But the odds could be longer than a cat's nine lives against Alice stopping a fast-shuffling pro from stacking the deck with one more death—which could be her own.

A CAT IN FINE STYLE

Alice Nestleton is putting on the dog: posing in elegant duds for a New York boutique's new ad. But she's surprised to find Bobbin, the clothes designer's once-beloved cat, exiled to the loft where the fashion shoot is taking place. Dressed-to-kill Alice stumbles across a corpse—the loft's wealthy owner, dead from an allergy to some gourmet pâté. Naturally the police call the death accidental. Just as naturally, Alice, with her nose for crime, smells a rat.

So when the victim's wife asks her to investigate, Alice calls on her boyfriend, Tony, to help unravel a thread of malice amid the secret affairs and shady transactions of the rag trade. But Alice's instincts tell her to *cherchez le chat.* What she finds may break her heart before she solves the top-of-the-line case involving a fat cat, clothes to die for, and murder by design.

Lydia Adamson is the pseudonym
of a noted mystery writer
who lives in New York.